THE GIRL WITH
2
HEARTS

THE GIRL WITH

2

HEARTS

T.T. THOMAS

BON VIEW
PUBLISHING

2014

THE GIRL WITH 2 HEARTS

Copyright © 2014 T.T. Thomas
Published by Bon View Publishing
All Rights Reserved
ISBN: 978-0-9862600-0-1

This book is a work of fiction. Names, characters, places, and incidents are a product of the author's imagination or are used fictitiously. Any resemblance to actual events, locales, or persons, living or dead, is coincidental.

Book Cover: Boulevard Photografica/Patty G. Henderson
www.boulevardphotografica.yolasite.com

Introduction and Acknowledgements

"It's been going on for centuries."

I have some people to thank, but most of them are dead.

They died in The Second Boer War, World I, World War II and all the wars, conflicts, operations, missions and troubles since. Before I wrote <u>The Girl With 2 Hearts,</u> I didn't know all that much about the Second Boer War, also called The South Africa War. But I had heard of it as I kept seeing references to it in my studies of World War I.

It turns out that, in a roundabout way, most of us have been both hurt and helped by the repercussions of that war. It began in 1899, ended in 1902 and in many ways set the stage for the kind of nationalism that enabled Germany to start World War I...and that we see to this day in our 21st century world.

Historians still debate what caused the Second Boer War, but most have acknowledged that at its most basic, it was a fight over gold, diamonds and slavery, and the land on which it all converged. In other words, it was about domination, power, influence and wealth.

The Boers were white European settlers of mainly Dutch ancestry who settled along the east coast of Africa. They eventually formed their own culture and had their own language, called Afrikaans.

The Dutch first came to Africa in 1649 when the Dutch East India Company sought refuge for rest and restoration for its crews and ships along the tea, spice and later, coffee trade routes. They would regroup in the coves and natural ports along the coast of what is today South Africa, particularly and initially at the Cape of Good Hope. There, as they eventually settled in the area, they did to the indigenous tribes of the Khoikhoi and the San what the British later did to them.

After numerous conflicts with the Boers, the British colonized the area and the fiercely independent Boers revolted. They fought over the area during most of the 1800s. Finally, in 1899 The Free Orange Republic and The Transvaal (South Africa Republic) joined to declare war on Great Britain.

The theme of the savage uselessness of war as a background for romance seems at once strange and perfect. When one is in the mud, rain, cold, and heat of war, and death is all around, love might be the only sane action taking place. Certainly, it must be one of the rarest and most life- affirming.

My prior novel takes place on the eve of World War I, also known as The Great War. For The Girl With 2 Hearts, we back up a bit to that transitional period between 1899 and 1902 when the cultural restrictions of the Victorian Age were about to give way to the more lenient societal elasticity of the Edwardian Era.

TGW2H is what I like to call Romantic Historical Fantasy...some romance, some history, some fantasy...even a little Magick. It mirrors some of the tones and themes of my other Historical Romances (The Blondness of Honey, Vivien and Rose, and A Delicate Refusal). Hopefully you will be transported to another time and place where you may find that who some of "us" are today, some of "us" were yesterday, too. I hope you enjoy the adventure!

With love, I thank my spouse, Karyn, for her unfailing

love, support, wisdom and responsiveness. This is especially true when I am in my writing mode, oblivious to dogs barking, cats meowing, doorbells ringing and the phone playing a rumba. Alone in the world, alone in my make-believe world. But it's no less true during those much-anticipated moments of togetherness where I interrupt movies, conversations, lovely dinners, etc., etc. with another 'what-do-you-think-of this?' idea for one of my books. She is irreplaceable as a partner, incomparable as home-sweet-home maker, and joyously human.

I can never repay fellow writers Patty G. Henderson and Ann Herendeen for their input, suggestions, edits— and an additional thank you to Patty for the gorgeous cover. These two women have been my Rock Solids on so many levels since my first published short stories and my first book, Two Weeks At Gay Banana Hot Springs. Both of them make me laugh, they make me write better, they make me happy.

I'd also like to thank my loyal readers, and I'd like to do it in person, at a great dinner, in Paris, followed by a trip to the top of the Eiffel Tower! Until then, however, I...uh...I've named a character after a few of you. More of you will materialize in the next book...I may change the spellings or permutations of names to protect your privacy, but remember, I'll always know who you are! Thank you from the bottom of my heart!

The Girl With 2 Hearts is just another love story between women with modern sensibilities at a time when modern was only modern relative to ancient. But there have always been women throughout history who fell in love with one another. It's been going on for centuries.

Why not in Queen Victoria's (family) world?

To my niece, my most favorite and only niece, Danielle E. Jacobs, the original girl with two hearts.

Queen Victoria is believed to have refused to pass a law banning lesbianism because she didn't believe there was such a thing as a lesbian, purportedly stating, 'Women do not do such things.'

From Many and Various Sources,
All of Whom Keep Repeating The Inaccuracies

First, any notion of her saying that has most certainly been determined by historians to be myth of monumental proportions.

Second, we suggest that what Her Majesty most likely said was the following:

"Women do not do such things frivolously; indeed, much thought and consideration goes into the decision, as well as in some, but not all cases, abundant planning, which may involve copious amounts of luggage and several phaetons. Beyond that, one suspects it would require an inordinate amount of sensitivity, appreciation and respect for the female body and heart for one woman to want sexual congress with another. Then too, and perhaps most importantly, when two women are in love, intimacy follows as night follows day; to suggest otherwise does not amuse us."

Of course, we may never know.

T.T. Thomas, Author
The Girl With 2 Hearts

The Girl With 2 Hearts

"We are not interested in the possibilities of defeat; they do not exist."

December 1899 letter from Queen Victoria to Arthur Balfour during the "Black Week" of the Boer War

<u>ONE</u>

Men can be so utterly dreary in their zeal for acknowledgement. Victoria Dormier looked over at her two brothers playing cards. Although they were on the other side of the room, she could hear their snickers and under-the-breath commentary. As usual, they were whispering about girls, between unremarkable hands. So boring. Utterly banal.

She reached for her well-worn copy of <u>Pride and Prejudice</u>. In fact, she mused, her whole life was becoming boring. She yearned for the lost freedoms of her relative youth. Or was that the relative freedoms of her lost youth? Nothing interested her brothers beyond the opposite sex. Even her beloved sister, Alexis, was more interested in securing a husband than seeking adventure. Not Victoria!

She travelled the world, in her mind, and visited natural wonders like Mount Everest in the Himalayas, The Sahara desert in Africa and the Sagano Bamboo Forest in

Japan, the Pyramids and The Hermitage—all places the interesting people had visited.

She met people from other cultures, ate their strange food, dressed in their colorful garb and even learned their language. She danced in Spain, she dined in France, she held court under white cotton canopies on apricot-hued verandas in Algeria and she slept in the arms of—uh, no one. Hmm. She fidgeted in her chair, twirled her deep chestnut hair absent-mindedly around her finger and opened the book in the large library of her father's substantial Kensington house.

She had just begun the opening paragraph of Jane Austen's classic when a loud commotion in the parlor brought all three of them out of the library into the hallway. She saw Jameson, her father's driver and another, younger man, helping her father to a chaise in the waiting room off the parlor.

"Father!" she cried. "What is it Jameson? What happened?"

Jameson explained how her father had fainted and fallen into the street behind the coach after exiting his solicitor's quarters. "I was atop the rig and didn't see him fall. Were it not for this young man..." he gestured vaguely in the direction of a man in patched clothing with a brilliant white scarf tied around his neck as a cravat. The clothing and the scarf were spotless. The young man stood up straighter.

Her father coughed a couple times and cleared his throat. "Lad saved my life."

"We'll call the physician," her brother said. "I'll get Mrs. Dann to fetch him."

After she saw to her father's comfort on the chaise, Victoria turned to the young man.

2

"And who might I be thanking?" she asked. "To whom do I owe my eternal gratitude?"

She smiled, but he maintained a somber visage. "Jack Pierce, ma'am."

"Mr. Pierce, may I offer you a cup of tea?"

"I think he should receive a monetary reward, Victoria!" her father said.

"No, sir, I cannot accept that. The cup of tea would be perfect though."

"Well, a letter, then, lad, of commendation. Worth more than money anyway. I'll have it done up tomorrow, and if you'll come 'round, I'll see you get it. And thank you, good fellow, thank you."

"Come into the library, Mr. Pierce," Victoria said. "My brothers will join us, and I'll have Charlotte bring us some tea and nourishment."

"There's no need, ma'am," Jack said sincerely. "I just came along to help the driver ensure your father's safe return. Anyone would have done as I have."

"Not anyone, son, not by a long shot," said her father, regaining a bit of strength. "Don't fully know what happened. One minute I was walking toward the carriage and the next I was being lifted into it. Damn shame about my new suit though." He looked over his torn pant leg and his dirty jacket. "Go on Victoria, your brother will see to me until the doctor gets here. Please show our good lad a nice tea."

Despite his inadequate apparel, Jack bowed smartly and turned to follow Victoria into the library. After she seated herself on a small divan, Jack waited to be invited. "Why not sit here, close to the warm fire?" she offered. He sat in a comfortable wingback club chair with a deep, plush seat.

They chatted amiably for over an hour with Victoria leaving the room only once to see about her father. She returned with a smile.

"He'll be all right," she said. "The doctor said perhaps he's caught a touch of croup, made him light-headed. They've put him properly to bed," she added.

Before her brothers came to join them, Victoria made polite inquiries as to Jack's residence, his line of work, or trade, and his family. He said he was an entrepreneur and lived in a let room near Marble Arch. He had no family, he offered. *Hmm. A single man not in possession of a good fortune, but still...*

She couldn't get over his handsome good looks. He was but an inch or so taller than her, but he carried himself with such presence that he seemed taller. His face was smooth shaven, his hair cut short but neatly and, most importantly, his hands were long and slender and his fingernails trimmed, clean and possibly a bit shined. He appeared not to be well off at all, but something about him suggested he ought to be. His accent was like hers, and his conversation was somehow both appropriate and humorous. She laughed several times. Her brothers, unfortunately, were less impressed with Jack, and while they were polite, the visit was soon over.

"I'll see to it that father's letter of commendation is ready for you tomorrow at four," she offered.

"It's really not necessary," he began, "but thank you."

She lowered her voice. "It's necessary I see you again," she said, her words tumbling over one another quickly.

He looked at her and seemed not to know where to put his hands. They were at the front door. With a bow, he opened the door himself. "Until tomorrow then," he said. As he walked down the front stoop, he paused, turned and smiled. A gorgeous, beautiful smile.

And that's how it began. Apparently.

TWO

She saw a large group of them at the far end of the alley warming their hands around a fire they had built in an old steel drum. She approached them but tiptoed in the black shadow of the dirty brick buildings that enclosed the narrow passage. Her eyes searched the faces illuminated by the flames. *He said he would be here. Doesn't mean he will be though.*

She paused and looked over the motley tag, rag and bobtail urchins posturing and posing bravely with their cloth-wrapped shoes, hand-me-down clothing and unscrubbed faces. They had little bodies and little teeth, if they had any teeth at all. Most were older than they looked, though. She knew that and eyed them as warily as they eyed her. Then the firelight revealed a pure white scarf with a perfect four-in-hand knot at the neck of Jack Pierce.

She raised her eyes to the glistening sparkle in his.

She watched as a slow, cynical twitch of his dimples fought to contain what would otherwise have been a wide smile. *Well, I'm sure he wants to smile. Naturally, he won't, in front of his mates. But he would. I think.*

"Ah, there you are, Pleasure," he said, looking at her. Unlike his friends, he spoke proper English when addressing her. His ease with the vernacular intrigued her: He parlayed, leveraged and invoked accent, dialect and idiom with advantageous, even pleasing, skill.

Several young men turned around and peered into the shadows from which Jack sauntered casually into the full light from the fire.

"Who've ye got, eh Jackie? A prop'r lady, innit!"

A chorus of guffaws and under-the-breath murmurs reached her ears. Jack moved around the circle as he raised his hand to quiet them.

I do wish he wouldn't call me Pleasure. It's not quite right in front of all these...ragamuffins.

"Jack," she said, lowering her eyelids. *Will he kiss me tonight? He seemed to want to last time...but oh, don't be a fool! I hardly know him. I know I'd let him though. Perhaps. All right, definitely.*

"Yes, Luv, I'm here. And there you are looking better than lovely, aren't you? Come into the circle, Treasure, warm your pretty hands now."

Well, I do prefer Treasure to Pleasure. For now.

She moved closer to the rusty barrel, but not too close. The flames licked the orange rusted vessel with an orange of their own. The boys' faces were flushed with the heat of the fire, but they stomped their rag-bound shoes to drive the freeze from their feet.

"Ay, Jackie's got 'is own fire, innit?" one of them crowed. "Jackie'll pass aroun' fags, now, an' 'av a smoke

7

wiff 'is mates, innit?"

She watched as Jack pulled a full tin of cigarettes from an inside pocket. She knew full well he'd do it to keep the boys from getting too rude. And to reaffirm his position relative to all of them. Jack stood up straighter, and she saw the droop of his ill-fitting jacket. He had a few rags wrapped around his right shoe, to keep the thin sole on the shoe, and his pants were patched, but he and his clothing were clean. The white silk cravat, though...'twas pure style.

With an ease that contradicted the tension in the air, Jack pulled a cigarette out, lit it, inhaled leisurely, then blew the smoke across the drum in a cloudy stream. They all watched him. Suddenly it seemed no one was breathing.

Jack held out his hand. "'Ere ya go, Mickie, an' pass 'em aroun'."

Mickie, a small boy with an eye patch, took the tin from Jack and proceeded to mimic Jack's actions before passing it around to the others. They all did it exactly as Jack had done. *But they aren't Jack.*

She and Jack took a position around the barrel, and the others stepped back a pace. They talked for a while, but she couldn't have said about what. She was smiling like an idiot. He was so handsome. She could have willingly drowned in the menacing depths of those deep brown eyes. His skin, darkened by the elements and burnished by the sun, looked smooth and soft in spite of both.

They had met nearly every night for the past two months. Sometimes here, sometimes at the other place near the river. She didn't recognize the other faces. They changed. Every time a different set of young transients.

But they all seemed to know Jack. She could see they respected him, too. He treated them each with evenness and a quiet strength. She saw that the deference seemed to give them a dignity they cherished as much for the source as the feeling. Jack made them feel this. Only Jack. To Jack they became and stayed loyal.

Snip-jacks, pickpockets and tawdry urchins to all they met, and to all who met them in darkness, they were like siblings to Jack. He was the soul savior of the mean street's young men, and a few girls, who dare not believe in being saved. Jack gave them hope. Of what they weren't certain, and for which they could as easily justify murdering him, but they didn't. To Jack they gave passage. She wondered why. And how he did it.

THREE

This was to be a special evening, and Victoria Dormier gathered up her patched pantaloons, her weskit, her scruffy boots, her raincoat and a floppy hat. Jack said they were celebrating his birthday, with some special treats and a bit of entertainment. She changed from her gown into the street urchin clothing in the privy near the kitchen, which was empty at this hour, with supper finished and the help gone to bed. She stuffed her gown, her brocade slippers and her jewelry into a large satchel hidden behind a cabinet, and then donned the wardrobe of her secret life.

She slipped out a side door of her father's house, ran across the empty street and met up with one of Jack's mates. Silently, he led her to a carriage that carried them both to the wharf.

The bonfire was extra large, and the boys passed around teacakes, cucumber finger sandwiches and canteens full of hot tea. Victoria wondered how they had managed the finger food but was impressed at how Mickie laid it all out nice and orderly on a clean cloth on one of the wooden casks.

Everyone seemed relaxed and jovial, and Victoria marveled, not for the first time, at how genuinely happy these lads were to be part of a small band of misfits. This was their family and despite their poverty, their outlaw station in life and their lack of education, they shared everything each of them had with one another. No one was left out, and Victoria saw a certain rough tenderness amongst them as they bantered about. They had a mysterious bond of civility and honor, even pride, as the older tended to the younger, the bigger looked after the smaller and the roughest kept an eye on the gentlest.

They all heard the agitated murmur of male scuttlers in the darkness at the end of the alleyway. Jack turned and peered into the darkness behind them. She looked too but saw nothing.

"Princess?"

She turned back toward him with a start.

"Princess, I must leave on an errand. I will be back in a flash. Five minutes. Mickie! Mickie, you're in charge and mind no harm comes to the lady. My lady."

Before she could say a word, he was gone.

He wasn't gone a full minute when she saw someone coming out of the shadows, in the opposite direction from where Jack had headed.

A fair-haired lad in a coat of many colors shuffled toward her, smiling. Well, it was somewhere between a smile and a sneer.

"Sorry, Luv, but I reckon he'll be delayed, innit."

"Jack? Why would he be delayed? He said five

11

minutes." She turned toward Mickie as if to confirm her report and saw him glaring at the intruder with his one good eye. "Well, I shouldn't be concerned," she added.

He nodded but slouched toward her. He wore a coat of long strips of colored cloth woven tightly into a weave that seemed to hold it all together while providing protection from the cold. The bottom of the coat was not hemmed, though, so it gave the effect of fringe.

"I see you fancy me coat, now, aye?" he said, leaning in closer to her ear.

She pulled back slightly but nodded again. "It's quite marvelous," she whispered. Then louder, "I do like it, actually."

"'Course it's not posh like yours, innit? But me mum made it 'fore I left home. Has sentimental value, innit."

He gave her an appreciative once over and then stepped closer. "Daft cold, innit?"

"Rather," she squeaked. *Oh, that sounded frail.* And then, in full voice, "Not too awful though. Could be rather worse!"

"Hmm. Rather agree," he said, trying to mimic her accent.

"Allow me to introduce m'self, m'lady. David Q. Dockwall, lately of Spitalfields." He held out his hand.

Spitalfields? *Oh my.* She had never been there, but she'd heard her brothers' friends speak of the sordid, wretched world of poverty and pain around Dean and Flower Streets.

She gave him her gloved hand and watched as he bent to kiss it. "Victoria," she said. "Very pleased to meet you."

"Are ye sure now? I might be the lad that steals you away from Jack when all's said and done, innit?"

Victoria blushed, but she managed a weak smile.

"Unless 'a course you be fond of soft skin and a pretty mouth like Jack's got," he challenged. Dockwall was handsome in a rough-hewn kind of way, and his manner was confident.

"Jack is a good friend of mine," she answered, trying to imbue her words with a slight tone of mild umbrage.

"Aye," mumbled Dockwall. "'Course there's far more to Jack than meets the eye, innit?"

"I'm sure I wouldn't know," she said, sniffing the air.

"For instance," he said, pulling a smashed cigarette out from the paper envelope inside his coat pocket. He lit the cigarette and slowly blew the smoke away from her face.

"For instance, I happen to know—"

"You know what?" said a voice behind them.

Victoria turned. "Oh, Jack, there you are!"

Jack met her eyes for a moment and then refocused on Dockwall.

"'Allo, Jackie, me boy," Dockwall said rubbing his hands together over the fire as if that gesture imparted warmth to Jack.

"David," Jack acknowledged.

"Ah 'twas nuthin' innit? Just a bit of gab going 'round about 'cha, me lad, and none of it true, I'm sure."

Dockwall took a long drag of his cigarette, and then tossed it on the ground before backing up a few paces. He stood with his arms folded. Victoria saw him widen his stance.

"Excuse me, Treasure," Jack said, leaning over to Victoria. He put his hands around her waist and in one smooth move placed her a few feet to the side from where they had been standing.

With his back still to Dockwall, he backed slowly away

13

from Victoria, let out an otherworldly grunt, pivoted on his left leg, and brought his right foot up squarely into Dockwall's, hmm, Dockwall's...ah, manhood.

Dockwall screamed with rage and pain. He curled up on the ground like a baby. Jack bent over him, then knelt down on one knee, his body blocking Victoria's view. He grabbed Dockwall's crotch and with a squeeze elicited a sad whimper.

"I think you've forgotten whatever it was you think you heard," Jack snarled. "Isn't that right, David?" With another hard squeeze, Dockwall half sat up to scream but unceremoniously puked instead. Jack leaned back from the mess and the smell.

"Oh dear, I do believe he has regurgitated his supper," Victoria mused, peering over Jack's shoulder.

"Step back, Luv, no sight for a Lady," Jack requested. Victoria stepped back and turned again to the fire sputtering in the iron drum. A half dozen young scuttlers looked at her wide-eyed but said nothing. She rubbed her hands together against the chill.

"Bastard," Dockwall choked out. "Bloody bastard."

Jack smiled. "Happy to hear you refer to me properly," he whispered. "Now, shut your trap, David, once and for all or my secret will die with your body, deep in the River Thames."

Dockwall coughed, spat and wiped his mouth on his already soiled coat. When he got his breath, he reached down to protect his groin with both hands. "She'll find out soon enough," he sneered. "But not from me," he added quickly when Jack's frown deepened. "But mind you, she will find out. A time will come, won't it, when even you won't be able to hide it." Dockwall laughed and his wicked eyes narrowed as the truth of it hung in the air between them.

Victoria heard that last bit. She wondered what it was she would find out. She couldn't imagine it would be much coming from the likes of Dockwall.

Jack lowered his voice. "Stifle it, David, or you'll not make it back to yer poor mum's tonight."

Victoria Dormier winced at the sudden turn toward violent encounter. She was troubled to see Jack so aggressive. It was the first time a shadow of doubt crossed her heart. As Jack said goodnight to all the lads, Victoria stood back and watched him. He was warm, affectionate and calming to his little band of outlaws. She watched them as they watched him. They clung to his every word, they nodded their agreement, they smiled their admiration. Nevertheless, she would have to find out what had brought forth such a physical attack between Jack and David. She sensed real anger between them, and yet she couldn't justify what she saw with the little bit that she heard. She was looking at Mickie as he drank down Jack's every word and gesture, but as she looked around, she saw Jack watching her. His somber visage told her that he knew something was unsettling her. A few moments later, he led her out of the alley.

Jack and Victoria walked for nearly an hour. "We're getting close to the posh part, Luv," Jack said. "I'm against sending you on alone from here."

"I'll be fine, Jack," she said, holding his arm tighter. "You'll watch as I get into the carriage."

They stopped and looked at one another. With a step backwards, they were in the shadows of the doorway to a closed shop.

"Jack," she said.

"Just trust me, Treasure. Trust me. Yes, I would like

to kiss you. But I won't. I won't as I know that we can never be more, my Blessing, though I'd give my life if we could."

"Jack," she murmured. She moved in closer to him.

It happened without a thought. It happened as though it were the most natural thing in the world. She initiated it, and when their lips touched, she felt as though she were kissing a warm cloud. His lips were soft, his face warm. And soft. Her own lips parted, as did his. She felt the shimmering charge course through her body, and she thought, yes, it seemed to have a similar effect on Jack. But Jack pulled back, gently, and touched her lower lip with his finger. They said nothing for a long moment, and he stared at her intently as if searching out the recesses of her very soul.

"An' I wonder what's my Flourish smilin' at, though I'm glad to see it whatever the' reason," he said. Unexpectedly, he smiled. An eyebrow arch suggested she answer.

She shook her head. "You have beautiful skin, Jack."

Jack laughed, his white teeth sparkling as if to match his tie. "A lad with pretty skin!" Jack exclaimed. "It's a right conundrum, then, isn't it, Sweetheart?"

She played with the fringe on her woolen scarf, glad that she had thought to wear it, glad that it gave her something to look at. *I shouldn't think he's quite earned the right to call me Sweetheart.* He reminded her of someone. That joy he has. She looked up at him, but his glance had moved across the street where three young men slouched half-hidden in another doorway. She saw a glint of warning as he stared in their direction.

"Who are they?"

"Just some mates, Treasure, just some mates." He

16

gave the group a small salute.

Hmm. Pleasure, Treasure, Flourish, Sweetheart. There was no denying: She liked them all. But she had to get something straight with Mr. Pierce first.

FOUR

"Speaking of mates, who is that horrid David Dockwall?"

"A problem," Jack admitted. He gave the group across the street the side eye. "And that lot over there are pals of his."

"So not really your mates, then?"

Jack looked at her, an upside-down smile creasing his handsome face. "I didn't want to worry you, Luv. That's all."

She nodded but felt the discomfort of a small tension between them. Jack put his arm around her waist and moved her onto the brick roadway, headed in the opposite direction of the group of young men. "Let's move away," he whispered. "And I will tell you all."

They walked a half mile or more before coming to a small park area well-lit by street lamps. A few carriages were lined up waiting for a fare. They stayed on the periphery of the park, in the brightest lit area. He led her to a stone bench. There were other couples around, walking slowly in the courtship stroll of lovers.

Jack pulled out his tin of cigarettes. "May I?" he asked politely. He bowed his head in acknowledgement when she nodded her accent.

"I know you prefer I not smoke—"

"In public, perhaps," she broke in, "but I do not mind so long as it is occasional."

"Thank you. Perhaps I'm a bit on edge this evening as I seem to need to smoke."

"Can you tell me about it, Jack?"

Victoria sat stone still after he finished. This was news he couldn't know was doubly treacherous to her personally. Another attempt on Queen Victoria's life was in the planning stages. Dockwall was involved, but he wasn't the leader. Jack didn't know who the leader was. Some anti-Royalist anarchist no doubt. Victoria had a hundred questions, but one repeatedly gnawed at her awareness.

"Jack...Jack, darling, how is it you have come to be in possession of this information?"

"Ah, my lady Victoria," he began.

Victoria blinked. *Oh, good heavens! I feel as though he knows me!*

"I keep a close eye on David Dockwall," he continued. "He's been trouble as long as I've known him. He's a bully, and he swindles people who haven't even as much as him. He cheats the lads, my lads, out of one thing or another."

Victoria nodded. She wondered what kinds of things Jack's little ragtags possessed. As if reading her mind, he offered an explanation.

"Sometimes, truth be known, my Angel, the lads pinch

things now and then. Usually a bit of fruit, or some tobacco, maybe a sweet now and then. Nothing very valuable and they always share with their mates. But if they are given something valuable...from a kind stranger or a fellow mate, such as a bit of money or a decent item of clothing, you can be sure Dockwall will try to steal it from them or worse, intimidate them into giving it to him. I'm not always around, Treasure." He paused and looked away. "As you know."

Oh, did she ever! He wasn't around nearly enough for her tastes. But they had a system, a system to keep her safe from wandering the streets looking for him. Sometimes she shivered in fear and excitement at the secret life she led.

Their system was simple. One of Jack's lads would stand across the lane from her father's house and doff his cap now and then, to no one in particular. That was the signal for her to meet Jack. She would see the messenger out of her bedroom windows, and if she dimmed the lamps, that meant she would be joining Jack as soon as she could successfully sneak out the side door near the kitchen. She had only to indicate her inability to join Jack a couple times, but those times broke her heart. Usually, she would find a way to join him. The messenger lad would wait for her across the street, and then lead her to Jack.

Sometimes there would be a gig waiting for her and the escort a block from her home when Jack was somewhere too far to walk. The carriage was always paid for by Jack, and more than once, Victoria wondered where he managed to acquire the kind of money such transportation would cost. But she never asked for fear of offending him. And she always thanked him.

"Do we have any information at all about the nature of this attack on...on our Queen?"

"A bit," he said. He looked around to ensure there were no eavesdroppers. "Apparently the Queen spends her Christmas holidays at Osborne House and—"

"Yes, she does, and her birthday and summer holiday and—" Victoria saw a frown dawning on Jack's face. "What is it, Jack?"

"No, nothing, sweetheart, nothing...just, you seem to know so much about the Queen."

Victoria feigned a laugh. "Well, she so rarely leaves Windsor, the newspapers make such a fuss when she does."

"That's true," he agreed. "Well, what I've learned is that another attempt will be made on her life somewhere between Windsor Castle and Gosport Terminus, before Her Majesty boards the extension rail to the Royal Clarence Yard. It has to be prior to reaching Gosport, I would think. Too much security once Her Majesty goes to the Yard to board the yacht."

"Could it happen on the water between the Yard and the landing at the Isle of Wight?"

"I can't imagine how! She's 300-feet long! The yacht I mean, not the Queen!"

Victoria's hand flew up to her face to hold back the laughter, but it was impossible. Jack smiled at her broadly, and then they both laughed. It was a good release of tension. They sat in silence for a few moments. She glanced at Jack and saw that he was deep in thought. In profile, he most resembled a Greek god. His high cheekbones, his patrician nose, his perfectly symmetrical face.

"But the more I think on it," he continued, "it might

just be the perfect place. Open water. Possible foggy weather. Few, if any, other boats around. The ship is its own defense, of course, but something smaller and faster could cause serious damage in an ambush."

"Or several somethings," Victoria offered.

Jack stood up and offered his arm. "I must see you home, my sweet one."

When Victoria took his arm, she felt his firm forearm and felt a shiver within. But when he rested her hand on his as they walked, she saw his slender fingers, his well-groomed fingernails, the complete absence of any weather-induced chapping or redness. She moved her hand in a slight rub against his, their arms entwined. His skin was actually as smooth and soft as her own. Indeed, hers might have been a bit rougher. As they approached the section of street where her carriage awaited her, Jack slowed.

A soft, slight rain began and the street-level fog began to rise. For a moment, though, they were hidden in a pocket of grey fog, the light of the carriage barely visible. Jack turned to her, lifted her chin with his index finger and peered into her night-darkened eyes. She couldn't see his, either, but she felt the brush of his lips against her cheek, at the corner of her mouth and then on her own lips. Their lips lingered in a sweet play of touch and barely touch until she pulled him closer, parted her lips slightly and encouraged him to explore. He pulled her close only to suddenly step back from her while still holding her arms.

"Victoria," he said, "you must leave. I...I..." He caught his breath. His forehead creased, and then he shrugged and smiled at the same time. "You are the moonlight upon my soul," he began, "and yet there seems no way ahead for us...no way at all."

It was her turn to take his face into her hands. "Shhhhh," she whispered. "You mustn't speak of all that. We must believe in destiny, and it feels as though ours is intractably intertwined."

She leaned into him and kissed him. He did not resist, but he did not respond. Victoria stepped into his arms and ran her fingers through his hair while she gently kissed him. "Shhhhh," she repeated. Whenever they got close, he would bring up the obvious class distinction. She understood, of course, but she couldn't help but sense there was more to his resistance than he said.

His arms gathered her into him, and they rocked back and forth for many moments. His hair was silky clean and baby fine. His barber had given him a most handsome styling in the manner of her father and brothers, she noted. Again, she wondered idly where funds for such grooming came from. Somewhere in their kiss goodnight she heard him say, "...Our destiny," but nothing more. No modifiers. No description. No pledge or promise. But it was enough for now that he repeated the important words.

FIVE

A few evenings later, Victoria looked out the window and saw the messenger.

About time! It's been three days!

There was something in the air when Victoria walked down the alley to join Jack and his band near the fire. Everyone seemed on high alert. The laughter was manic, the conversation curt and no one seemed to want to make eye contact with Victoria.

Behind them, they heard a huge roar. An apparition appeared on a motorbike in black leather helmet, doublet and an outer jacket with bright metal buckles for closure down the front and around the collar and the wrists. The dark intruder pulled up to Jack's group, shut the engine and removed a pair of goggles. Victoria's mouth fell open, but her gaze was transfixed when the rider pulled off the cap to reveal a shock white head of hair. Each strand of hair seemed to stand on point, spiky, short and shimmery.

"Ah, Deeci!" Jack called out. "Wondered where you

were."

Deeci? And he wondered?

Her heavy boots clumped up to Jack. She chucked a couple fingers under his chin and grinned as she gave Victoria the once over.

"Did you now, Luv? Likewise, I'm sure."

Victoria had never seen Jack nervous. He stumbled over his words. "Oh, uh, right, uh, Victoria Dormier may I introduce Diesel Archer?"

Diesel. What? Have I misheard?

Deeci stuck out her hand. "Charmed, I'm sure."

Victoria held out her hand, palm down, and Deeci laughed. "Well, then, Your Grace." She grasped Victoria's hand and gave it a sturdy shake.

Is she kidding? Where's the rest of the fingers of her gloves? Ow!

"Hello," Victoria said.

Diesel smiled. Even in the shadows, Victoria could see her green eyes. And she had dimples, not unlike Jack's. Victoria was mesmerized; she had never seen a face like Diesel's. Alabaster white skin, kohl-outlined eyes. Astonishingly, her lips were painted green, and her mouth seemed set in a semi-permanent sneer. And yet, when she smiled fully, hers was an open, sensuous face that looked like it could launch ships or sink the Navy.

Diesel turned to Jack. "So, Jack, thought we might go for another ride sometime soon. When you're not busy," she said, her eyes penetrating his.

"Of course, Deeci, we will. And soon."

You will not. Not sooner or later. She looked down at the knee-high black boots, each one emblazoned with a large "D" for the buckle.

"I'm counting on it, I'm sure," Diesel said. "I see ya

there, Mickie! Being a good boy?"

Mickie shrugged. "Givin' it a try, now and then, innit."

"That's the spirit!" Diesel said. She turned again to Victoria. "Eh, d'ya ride, Victoria?"

Victoria couldn't believe it was her own voice. "Of course."

Diesel looked at Victoria's clothing. "Eh, well, one challenge at a time, I reckon."

Excuse me? Is she ridiculing me? But she looked closer at Diesel's outfit, memorizing every piece. With nothing to add, Victoria gave a slight nod and then looked at Jack for guidance. He nodded knowingly but said nothing.

"Right, well Diesel Archer will be off now!" Diesel announced.

As Diesel climbed aboard and pulled on her leather helmet, Jack touched Victoria's arm reassuringly before walking over to Diesel. Victoria leaned in to hear better.

"Have you looked into what we spoke of?" Jack asked.

"I have, and we need to discuss it," she said.

He nodded while she put her goggles on. She glanced over at Victoria.

"Mind you'll have to switch from blue blood to red, Jackie Luv."

All the little guttersnipes began a slow clapping that changed up into a faster rhythm once the goggles went on. Jack did not join them in their applause.

Some heathen ritual, one supposes.

Diesel began to chant. "I go through things, not around them! I jump through doors, I don't pound them! I ride like the devil and kiss like an angel, I—"

"All Right, Deeci, all right!" Jack said. "Enough boys! Good ride, Deeci!" he called out.

26

Jack shook his head and turned to walk back to Victoria. As he did, Victoria saw that Diesel was looking directly at her. Leaning toward Jack and pulling him toward her for a kiss on the cheek, Victoria looked right back at her. Diesel laughed and roared away into the blackness of the night.

Jack rubbed his hands together and held them out palms up over the fire. "An old friend," Jack said.

"Who? Oh, you mean Diesel? A family name, Diesel?"

Jack laughed. "Believe it or not—

Try me.

"Her name was supposed to be Giesel, it's a German form of—"

"I know what it's a form of," Victoria said. "Gisele. I rather think it's best they got it wrong."

Jack looked at Victoria. "Well, Treasure, I suspect you're quite right."

Time to go home now.

As they walked the long route to the waiting carriage, Victoria discovered that Diesel, Jack and another friend or two rode their bikes throughout the night when Jack's crew was most likely to be set upon by the likes of David Dockwall's lads. Apparently, Jack's crew was on the small side, in number and physical build. His was one of only a handful crews to include girls, of which there were several.

"Each member of my crew has a specialty," he said, continuing the conversation.

Victoria was doing a slow steam about Diesel, but she decided to keep it to herself, for now. "A specialty? Such as?"

"Treasure, when we spoke of attempts on the Queen's life, our intelligence told us it was to be around the holidays. Now we're hearing it may be sooner. Very soon. I think you've guessed about me, haven't you, Treasure?"

Noooooo. No. No. I haven't guessed anything!

When she didn't answer, he explained.

"I'm actually quite involved in espionage," he said, "and this lot are my street team. All informants. Plus, we have two technicians who keep the transportation equipment in top shape at all times. Then we've got moles and—"

"Moles? What an odd word!"

"Well—they're our spies who have infiltrated the enemy camp."

"This all sounds quite villainous and even dangerous," Victoria said.

"It is, Luv, it is. But my work is important to...to certain authorities, and all these lads and lassies back me up."

"Is that what Diesel is? A backup?"

"She is, Treasure. And a good one."

"What does she do?"

"She kills," Jack said, "but only when necessary."

"Good Lord, Jack, why would she do that? Kill anyone?"

"She has to, Luv, to protect me and the crew. These others...these others aren't just common petty thieves," Jack said. "They're anarchists. Out to do...out to do serious damage to our government."

Victoria immediately understood. Anarchists were especially fond of trying to kill Auntie. She heard her father say it many times, and several times lately. They hated the Royals, loathed the government, held rallies to show their disdain for any societal restrictions whatsoever and weren't overly fond of tradition and sentimentality.

"My group...well, it's high up," he said. "I'm not

allowed to divulge. Even the crew doesn't know what we really do, not fully."

They stopped walking for a moment, and stepped inside a doorway overhang to let a carriage pass.

"So you're not really a...a..."

"A what, Treasure?"

Victoria swallowed. "A pauper?"

Jack turned to her and raised his finger to her cheek, his visage obscured by the shadows around them. His gaze travelled from her lips to her nose to her eyes. "No."

Victoria felt as though he had answered a different question. One she hadn't asked.

"Jack, I want to join you. You and your posse. I don't think I can kill anyone, but I'm...I'm in a position to perhaps obtain information. And I've driven my brother's Singer bike!"

Jack smiled. "Our motorbikes are a bit more powerful than the Singer," he said. "They are custom, made especially for me...and Diesel."

Oh, forget about Diesel for a moment!

"I see," she said.

Victoria leaned in. She closed her eyes, but her lips sought out his. When they touched, she felt a strange flush course through her body. His lips were firm but soft. The kiss lasted far longer than she had intended. Far longer. When her tongue touched his glistening white teeth, they both jumped.

Sorry! Uh, actually, no, not sorry!

As Jack stepped back into the street and gave her his arm, he looked over at her. "Let me think about it. No promises, but..."

That's all Victoria Dormier wanted to hear. She held her body close to his as they walked.

SIX

It all happened faster than Victoria anticipated. First, a letter arrived at her home advising her that she would be picked up by a Miss Archer at around midnight. She hastily tore up the letter and paced around her room for a quarter hour. After lunch, she announced a headache and told everyone she was going for a long nap. Dinner was to be sent up to her. Her father was on some business at their country house. Her brothers were home, but would be out at their clubs in the evenings. Alexis was spending hours with her dressmaker and some of her theater friends.

Just before midnight, Victoria slipped through the kitchen and out into the service quarter porch. No one would be using the door to the outside until morning, so she went through the usual routine of placing a folded up piece of paper between the lock and the door jam to ensure quick and easy re-entrance. Suddenly she heard the unmistakable sounds of a motorbike. She peered out the window of the porch and saw that Diesel had stopped about a half block from the Dormier house. She watched as Diesel doused the headlight.

"Evening, Your Grace," Diesel said, as Victoria approached.

"Hello Diesel."

Diesel looked her up and down and shook her head.

"What? What's wrong?" Victoria said.

Diesel starred at her for a few beats and then stepped on the starter. Over the roar, Victoria heard "Just about everything, your Grace, just about everything. Hop on."

Victoria climbed on the back and instinctively grabbed Diesel around the waist when the bike took off.

"Put your knees up," yelled Diesel.

Bloody hell!

"What?" yelled Diesel.

"Nothing!" Victoria shouted. "Where are we going?"

"Shopping," said Diesel.

They drove through thick banks of fog and up hills to a view of clear skies. They seemed to be taking the scenic route as Diesel stormed past Parliament and other government buildings, finally coming to a stop in the well-lit, colorfully populated Piccadilly area. Diesel pulled up in front of a storefront and cut the engine.

Victoria climbed off the bike and stumbled. Diesel, still astride the bike, reached out and grabbed her.

"Don't kill yourself in that get-up," she said, indicating Victoria's poor urchin costume. "Be an embarrassment to your family name."

"Leave my family name out of this," Victoria said.

Diesel laughed and climbed off the bike. "Follow me."

"Where are we going?"

Diesel said nothing but walked quickly around to the

31

back of the storefront. She knocked twice and the door opened. "Got a real challenge for you lot," Diesel said. "Have her ready in two hours."

The two women at the door frowned as they looked Victoria up and down. "This one will be extra," a blowsy blonde said.

"This one will be double," the redheaded one said.

"Fine," said Diesel. "Just have her ready. See you in a couple hours, Your Grace."

Victoria was pulled inside the shop by one of the women, and she walked down a long hallway to a door.

"What's this?" Victoria asked.

"Think of it as a spa," said the redhead.

***

Diesel pulled up a little early, turned off the bike and stood beside it smoking. After a quarter of an hour, she noticed a couple of women standing about 30 feet away. They seemed to be involved in their own conversation, and paid her no attention, so she waited. She was facing the door at the rear of the storefront. Finally, she threw down her cigarette, stomped over to the door and knocked twice. The redhead opened the door.

"You're late," Diesel said.

"No, you're late, she left here 20 minutes ago."

"What kind of—"

"Over there," the redhead said, pointing at the two women Diesel had seen earlier.

Diesel turned around as a young woman in thigh-high boots, black leather, black lip coloring and short, black, spiked hair and a face powdered up like a geisha walked toward her.

32

"Kitty got your tongue, Diesel?"

"Victoria? I don't believe it!"

"I was just getting rather fond of 'Your Grace,'" Victoria said. "Let's go, I think Jack is waiting. For me."

***

They met Jack in a large empty armory near Hyde Park. As she and Diesel approached, Victoria saw a group of about twelve people through one of the soot-encrusted windows, a dim yellow light providing the only source of illumination for the dark, brooding structure. She saw four or five motorcycles parked near a wide door, but one in particular caused her to slow down. It was bright red and big. Black leather saddlebags were slung over the rear fender, and a big black seat of softest, plump cowhide bridged the bike. Its pipes were blindingly bright silver metal and it had something Diesel's bike did not: footrests for the passenger.

"Jack's," said Diesel.

"Thought so."

Jack was speaking to the small assembly. Diesel walked in first and went to the left to an open seat. Victoria stood perfectly still once inside. It took a moment for her to focus her eyes, and when she did, she realized they were all looking at her. And Jack had stopped speaking. He stared at her and she at him. When recognition dawned, his slow smile beckoned her forward. She walked straight through the crowd and up to the large table where Jack stood alone.

"Treasure," he said, pulling out a chair for her.

A slight nod. No words.

He bent over as he pushed her chair in from behind.

"You look ravishing," he whispered. "Stunningly, breathtakingly gorgeous."

Again, no smile. But she did wink.

***

When they pulled up across from her house, she dismounted and reached over to touch his arm. A soft, light rain made her move into his arms. As they kissed, he slipped his free arm inside her jacket. She felt the pressure from his fingertips as he moved his hand in a circular motion on her back. When he touched skin, she wanted to crawl back up on the seat, but facing him.

Oh Lord. This can't go on!

The rain increased and within seconds, it became a downpour. She pulled away.

"Goodnight, love."

"Sleep well," he said. "You." She ran across the street as he called out. "Oh! Victoria, your face!"

She smiled as she sprinted away from him. Sleep well You, too.

Victoria managed to slip in through the service porch door silently. Once inside the porch, she undressed, put her new gear into the satchel, stashed it behind the cabinet and slipped into her dressing gown and robe. She walked through the kitchen and ran smack into Alexis, who screamed to high heaven.

Victoria waved her arms wildly, which only seem to unhinge what last vestige of restraint Alexis had as she cowered behind her own arms.

"Shhhh. Alexis! Be quiet!"

"Victoria? Oh my God! What happened to your hair! What happened to your face?"

34

"Do you like it?"

"Oh my God! Oh my God! Father will have a heart attack! Why?"

"Alexis, please calm down. It will grow back!"

"But it's bbbbbblllaaaaaccccckkkkkk!"

Alexis pulled her sister over to a small looking glass above a kitchen cabinet. All of the white makeup had run, run for its life down her cheeks, her nose, her chin. Unfortunately, so had the black hair dye, leaving patches of brown all over her head and lines of soot on her face. *Oh my. That is frightening.*

"I see your point, Alexis."

"You look like a zebra who got mixed up with a brown bear!" Alexis said.

Victoria took her sister's hand to lead her up to their bedrooms, but Alexis pulled back.

"I was...hmmm...a bit hungry."

They both turned and headed for the icebox. Giggling, they rummaged up some cheddar cheese and slices of cold meat. They pulled apart the remains of a French roll, slathered it with butter and ate silently, except for noises and moans of pleasure.

"Do I dare ask?" asked Alexis, wrapping up the remaining cheese.

"Not yet, darling," cooed Victoria, "but soon. I think. Just trust me, sister. I'm working for the Monarchy."

"Does Auntie know?"

"Not exactly."

"Oh Lord," said Alexis. "Come on, let's get to bed before I regret this chance meeting in my own kitchen with a bohemian of appalling appearance, uncertain lineage and truly desolate future!"

Victoria grinned. "I rather like the sound of that!"

Just as they rose from the table, they heard shuffling, and their brother Ambrose entered the room.

"I say, who's—oh sorry," he said as he came through the door, "I didn't realize you had company, Alexis."

Victoria sat back down, covered her face with her hands and kept her head down.

"Oh, Brosie! Just sitting here with my theater friend having a snack with me. Afraid she's got an awful headache though."

Ambrose looked at Victoria, frowned and unwrapped the cheese. "Ah, sorry about that. Just have a bite of this and leave you ladies to visit." He took a large piece of cheese, stuffed in his mouth and turned to leave.

"Hope that headache improves," he said, turning toward Victoria. "Have we met?"

Alexis jumped up and began clearing the table again. "No! Sorry, Ambrose, this is my friend...my friend Donella."

Victoria managed a pinky finger wave but kept her hands over her face and said nothing.

"Right, well, good night, ladies."

They waited until they heard him reach the top of the second-floor landing before doubling over in laughter.

"My own brother," said Victoria. "I always knew I was a stranger in my own home."

"Oh, pshaw! He's half asleep, and you look...foreign."

Victoria grinned. "Donella?"

Alexis shrugged. "A friend of my friend Nancy, who's actually a friend of my dear old friend Mary. Rest in peace."

"Oh. Did she pass on?" Victoria yawned.

Alexis dismissed further conversation with a wave. "Yes and no. Some other time, then."

<u>SEVEN</u>

Victoria sat in her room with an old wig of her mother's placed haphazardly on her head. The white makeup on her face had been a bit difficult to remove, but some cold cream did the trick. It was just past noon, but she was sleepy. *This charade of identities is exhausting! Still, Jack seems...Jack seems to adore the new me.* She fell asleep for three hours, and arose just in time for dinner. No one said a word about her hair, but she almost fell off her chair when Ambrose inquired about Alexis' friend.

"Did Donella's headache ease?"

"Who? Oh. Yes, yes it did."

Ambrose barely concealed his sniff of disapproval. "I didn't realize you had theater friends," he said.

"Oh, Brosie," Victoria said, "You are such a dear old crusty. For such a young man, I mean."

"Well, you say that," he said, "but you should have seen her. Looked like something out of a Wilkie Collins novel."

"I adore that look," said Alexis, buttering her roll. "It's all the rage now."

"In some quarters, I'm sure," Ambrose said. "Probably shouldn't introduce her to Papa, though."

Victoria raised her fork. "Daddy is far more unconventional than you give him credit," she said. "Indeed, I don't know where you get your snobbishness."

Ambrose twisted his mouth into a shrug. "Well, I get it from Auntie," he said. "And don't point with your utensils."

When he wasn't looking, but Alexis was, Victoria picked up her knife and did a fast air carving of Spring-Hill Jack's signatory "S."

***

Diesel picked Victoria up at midnight, and again they met with Jack, only this time in a small wood near the train station.

"You look even better than before," said Jack, taking both of Victoria's fingerless-gloved hands and bending low to kiss them.

Victoria's mouth twisted into a combination pout and shrug. "You didn't tell me my face makeup had run down my face."

"I did try," Jack said. "But you had already run across the street. Besides, you were adorable."

I'll take 'adorable.'

They waited for two others, and then Jack held up his hand for silence. "We've a serious problem, mates. The big

38

anarchist rally is in about an hour. I know from my crew that Dockwall and his mangy group will be there, but we're fairly certain they will leave to attend a private meeting. That's the part where we're light on details."

"Do we know where the meet-up might be?" asked Diesel.

"We do. Well, we think we do. Odds are for the old bridge works building near the Tower Bridge. But there's two large buildings and a half dozen smaller ones. We think the meeting is on the north side in the bigger of the two big buildings."

"How do we get in even if we do know which building?" said a big burly man carrying a helmet with horns attached.

"We don't," said Jack. "Everything we know so far tells me they will try to..." he glanced at Victoria, "...try to pull off a hit next Sunday."

"Sunday?" Victoria said. "Sunday is when the Royal household goes through the park." She looked at Jack for further explanation.

"Yes, Treasure, it is. We don't know for sure who the target is, but it's someone in the Monarchy."

Victoria's shoulders slumped. "It's the Queen," she said. "Has to be."

"We have to be ready for anything."

"Well, shouldn't the Palace be told so they can alter their Sunday driving plans? Like canceling them?"

"We need to catch these people," Jack said. "They're getting bolder and more dangerous."

Victoria raised an eyebrow. *No kidding.*

Jack paced around the small area, slipping into shadows and back again. Everyone was quiet.

"The problem now is that we have no way for our two

moles to get that close," he said from behind a tree. Victoria looked in the direction of his voice but couldn't see him. She glanced around the eerie woodland hideout and shivered as she wondered if any eyes other than Jack's were looking back at her.

"Nobody here," Jack said, walking out from under the tree.

Oh, my. He thinks as I do. But he's so brave, so willing to take a risk...

"I'll go in," she said.

"No, Treasure. It's too dangerous. Besides, you've already met Dockwell."

"Not looking like this!" she said. "My own brother didn't recognize me from two feet away. I can do this. And it's all dangerous, Jack. I'm part of it now."

"She's right, Jack," Diesel said. "She could get close to Dockwall at the rally. He's a sucker for a good-looking woman."

Victoria looked at Diesel, gave a modified curtsy and mouthed a 'thank you.' Diesel rolled her eyes and held back a smile.

After watching that exchange, Jack looked at the ground. "All right, but we'll have you in our sight the whole time at the rally. You'll be on your own until we get to the waterworks. If that's where the meeting is."

"Can't she signal us if we've got it wrong?"

Victoria answered. "I can, and will." She pulled a short white scarf out of an inside pocket of her leather jacket. It was a shorter version of Jack's scarf but just as white, just as fine a silk. She took in his look of surprise and approval, and continued. "If we have the location right, I'll put the white scarf on...this way." She tied the scarf around her neck with the knot in the front. "If I don't know where the meeting is, I'll put it on this way." She moved the knot around to the back of her neck.

"On one condition," Jack said. "If you don't know where the meeting is, you have to manage to give Dockwall the slip. Stay around the rally. Look for the big Marxist book tent. We'll find you around there."

Victoria nodded. "One has to hope."

EIGHT

It didn't take Victoria long to spot Dockwall once Jack had left her in an area of the weekly rally he was known to frequent. She saw him talking to a couple young women, but he was surrounded by a half-dozen young men with varying degrees of menace about them. Varying from wildly menacing to deathly menacing.

A most unattractive group I must say.

Victoria watched Dockwall out of the corner of her eye. When she knew he had focused in on her, she purposefully turned away so her profile was to him. She stayed standing where she was. She pulled a cigarette out from where it was lodged in a strap on the outside of her jacket sleeve and put it in her mouth. She looked around as if for a light.

"Might I light that for you, now, Beauty?"

She put her face down into his cupped hands, and when she pulled up, she gazed at him through the puff of smoke she exhaled.

"Nice," she said.

"Nice?"

"Nice name for someone you don't know."

"We could change that, Beauty. I'm having a party later...care to come?"

"Not really," she said as she took another puff. She looked around and made eye contact with some random young man in round glasses.

"Ah, I see you prefer the intellectual type, eh Beauty?"

Victoria turned to look at Dockwall. He had a nice smile so long as you didn't know the black heart behind it.

"I prefer the exciting type," she said evenly. "Are you that type?"

Dockwall nodded, but a shadow of wariness crossed his visage. "Never saw you around before."

"New in town," she said. "I've been in Russia for the past year."

Dockwall's eyebrows shot up. "Russia! Always wanted to go. They know a thing or two about the common man."

Jack saw that Victoria had snared Dockwall, and he watched as the two of them talked for a while. Soon Victoria moved off with Dockwall, and even allowed him to lightly hold her elbow as guidance. They walked to the periphery of the large street gathering and ducked into a small cafe. Jack got out his spyglass, but the windows of the cafe were steamed up. He could see they had got a table, but once they sat down, he could see nothing. He smacked his palm repeatedly with the spyglass.

"Just relax, Jack. She'll be fine," Diesel said.

As they waited in the shadows of a side street, Jack never took his eyes off the front door of the cafe. After an hour, he saw them come out. Victoria was wearing her scarf with the knot at the front.

"It's the water works building, all right!" he said to the others. "Let's go!"

Jack and his crew watched from a small hilly street above the rally, and within a few minutes, they saw Dockwall and two dozen riders head in the direction of Tower Bridge. Sitting behind Dockwall, Victoria was a spooky specter. "He's sure loving that," said Jack, grinding out a cigarette with his boot.

Diesel dismounted and pulled a small crossbow out of her side bag.

"Ah, you can't be thinking you're going to need that tonight," Jack said.

"No, just checking it." She held it up and examined the line of sight. She twisted a couple metal screws, and then returned it to the saddlebag.

"Right. Well, go on now, and if there's the slightest indication he won't be returning with her here, put Mickie on the Tower Bridge train to come tell me. I'll wait here, and when she gives him the slip, I'll pick her up."

Jack rolled down the hill with his crew, and they left their bikes at a horse stable near the edge of the streets bounding the rally area. They walked the edge of the fair, but Jack was nervous. He was looking in every direction, and he stared extra hard at certain people. They hadn't spent more than an hour when he looked up and saw Victoria walking toward him. He turned around when he was sure she saw him and walked in the opposite direction, toward the bikes. When she reached him, he grabbed her hand.

"Tell me you're all right," he said.

"I'm all right. I didn't even have to give him the slip, just told him my aunt and uncle were waiting for me at a pre-arranged spot."

"And he bought it?"

"Of course, he bought it," Victoria said. "Besides, after what I found out, I didn't want to risk him catching me in a lie and have the whole thing change."

He drove her home, but stopped a half block from the service porch. They both got off the bike and stepped back in the shadows of the trees.

"It's big, Jack. It's my...it's the Queen. And it's Sunday."

Jack nodded, but he seemed preoccupied. "But you're...you're all right? He didn't...didn't try...didn't...?"

Victoria gave him a look. "No, darling, he did try...to sound intelligent and worldly, but he's just not."

Jack didn't say anything, but the way he was gnawing on his own lower lip told her he was full of angst. "What could that heathen possibly have to talk about for an hour?"

Victoria knew he couldn't see her smile. She took his hand. "So, Jack darling, you're not..."

Jack's head snapped up. "Not...what?"

"You're not perturbed with me, are you darling? I did what we needed, didn't I, darling?"

He moved in closer. With his right hand, he took her short black spiky hair in his open palm and pulled her firmly into a kiss. This time, no one jumped back. In fact...when tongues touched...and they, uh, they did touch, Victoria reached up and put her arms around Jack's neck, pulled his head down and fashioned some serious kissage. Afterwards, she used her finger to rub off the black lip coloring that had transferred from her mouth to his.

"Can't have you looking like a girl," she said before darting across the street.

Jack watched as she walked the half block to her home. With a sigh, he touched his lips.

NINE

There was one casualty on Sunday, but it wasn't the Queen. Her Majesty's Sunday drive went off as planned, and several members of the Royal family followed along in their carriages. Lenchen rode with her mother, and although they marveled at the unseasonably good weather, both soon tired of waving and asked to be taken home for an early tea.

The Dockwall gang was stopped before they even got astride their motorcycles by a barrage of dangerously close arrows from someone's crossbow raining down on them from a nearby hill. When one of the troublemakers was hit in the leg, the whole group dispersed. Dockwall was the first to flee.

Diesel turned to Jack and grinned. "Happy now?"

Jack leaned over and gave her a kiss on the cheek. "Yes, Deeci, I'm very happy."

"Well, good, because I'm off to America. Next week."

"You don't have to leave, Deeci...I still need you as part of my—"

"Crew? I know. But you'll be fine. And I'll be back for visits. Probably."

Jack walked up to Diesel and pulled her in for a hug.

"All right. Will you write me? I'll want to know...that you're well, as I'm certain you will be."

"Sure. Sure, I'll drop you a line now and then." She turned to mount her bike. Once on it, she pulled her helmet on, adjusted her goggles, pulled her jacket tight and revved the engine."

"Goodbye, Jack."

"Goodbye, Diesel."

"No regrets," she said as the bike began to roll.

"No regrets," he agreed. "Deeci?"

"Yes?"

"Thank you."

She threw her head back in a half nod and roared away.

Mickie and the others were a ways down the path from Jack but sauntered toward him.

"Where's Diesel going, Jack?" Mickie said.

"She'll be back," he answered.

Mickie looked after the cloud of dust thrown up by Diesel's bike. "Yeah, she'll be back, innit."

***

After Deeci had gone, Jack went back to his pauper trappings.

"We're going to stay out of leather and off our cycles for a while," he had said to Victoria. "The Queen's security detail has been beefed up, and whoever's giving orders to Dockwall will want to lay low for quite a while, maybe months."

Fine with me, this hair is a mess and the wig is in tatters. And Daddy is returning later this week.

They met at the usual place, and Victoria noticed that Jack seemed in another world. He wasn't distant, but he was not his usual spirited self, either.

They left the group earlier than usual and took a walk.

"Are you concerned about Mr. Dockwall being on the loose?" she asked.

"No, Treasure, not really. He won't be pursuing murder for a while, now he knows we're onto his schemes. But he might try something different. He might even try to find you."

"Me? Whatever for? He surely knows I led you right to him!"

"No, my sweet, he knows that some bohemian woman with coal-black hair, a ghost-white face and tree-green lips led me to him!"

"Hmm. I suppose you're right. Well, he won't find me, will he!"

Jack stopped walking and led them into an alcove of a closed storefront.

"I hope not because...Victoria?"

"Yes, Jack?"

"I think I'm...that is, it seems, uh, we do seem quite suited to one another don't we?"

Victoria moved into him and whispered. "Yes, darling, I believe we are."

No one said anything.

Next sentence, please. Hello? Yoohoo? Anyone here want to tell me they're falling in love with me?

Nothing. *Right. Here goes. I can handle this.*

"Jack, will you tell me your secret? The one that Mr. Dockwall and you spoke of?"

"In time, yes, I suppose I must, but, for now, does it matter, my heart?" he asked leaning in closer to her. His lips brushed her cheek, his warm breath covered her ear and she felt a charge course through her body.

Does what matter? Whatever it is, I'm ready. Her breathing quickened, her face grew hot. *But he's just talking about his mates. Surely, he...*She reached up and touched his cheek. So soft. So warm. She looked deep into his eyes and as the twinkle within shone a light too bright to ignore, she realized he had...pretty eyes, pretty, long, dark eyelashes, pretty...everything.

"I fear you've guessed it after all," he whispered. "Does it matter, my Anguish, does it matter so much?"

It might have been the heat from the closeness of their bodies or it might have been the chill from an overabundance of emotional confusion, or it might have been the thrill of perplexing mystery, but Victoria Regina Dormier, 65th heir to the throne of England by virtue of her Aunt, Queen Victoria, fainted into the arms of Jack Pierce.

Apparently, something mattered.

TEN

Jack carried her the short distance to the waiting carriage. The driver was standing alongside his coach. Except it wasn't the usual driver. Jack stopped, visibly shocked.

"What have you done to Lady Victoria, lad?" he asked, his voice revealing anger and alarm.

"To? Sir?" Jack feigned confusion.

"Lady Victoria, and for God's sake don't drop her lad. Here, help me place her on this seat." He whipped open the carriage door and stepped inside to receive the limp body. Victoria began to rouse, but she was confused.

"Jack? Jack? Benson, Jack is a friend, it's all right..."

"There now, milady, just rest a spell. Sit back, please."

"Sir! I cannot allow the lady to leave my presence with a stranger!"

As the driver positioned Victoria inside the carriage, Jack could see its appointments were rich and supple.

The driver stepped out of the carriage. He stopped and turned to Jack.

"I am the Queen's personal Private Secretary, and I suggest you disappear, Mr. Jack. Before the entire court of Her Majesty arrives to take you to the dungeon for causing bodily harm to a member of the Royal family." *However distant, he mumbled.* "Now go!"

Jack backed away from the coach. How had this man known where he would bring Victoria?

He turned to retrace his steps but saw two Dockwall lads hovering in the doorway and changed his mind. Using the carriage as his cover, he turned and ran in the opposite direction. He ran and ran and ran.

Finally, he stopped, out of breath and out of hope to ever be near her again. Tears and perspiration covered his face with a stinging sheen. He should have known this would get complicated. She was too special, too different, and yet, so like him. He should have told her the truth early on. He wished he had never met her. They had her father to blame for that misfortune, not that it mattered now.

He walked along the river path, in and out of fog clouds that covered his shoes. He couldn't go home, and he couldn't see Victoria Dormier again. He was useless to the Crown, now, he reasoned. He couldn't serve Her Majesty as Royal Liaison, a euphemism for spy, because he was falling in love with Her Majesty's niece! As for his inheritance of title...Ha! Not as Jack Pierce.

Dockwall, scum that he was, had a point: If Jack didn't divulge his secret to Victoria, then she'd come upon it soon enough herself. She seemed to be getting close. She didn't realize it, of course, but it was only a matter of time. It mattered not that the Queen already knew his secret and had asked him to use his compelling and believable disguise to her own royal advantage. Falling in love with her niece, though? Umm, no. That was guaranteed to upset the royal temperament in a rather huge way.

And then Benson. He must have been following Victoria. But for how long? Was tonight the first time? When it all came crashing down, and he felt it would, he'd be out of luck, out of love and out of a job. The Queen would never trust Jack Pierce again. For that matter, neither would Victoria Dormier.

Jack leaned over the low stone wall of Windsor Bridge to catch his breath. He feared he might retch, the roiling in his stomach vying for attention with the throbbing in his temple and the rapid beating of his heart. The Thames was dark and churning. Swollen by the recent rains, the river flowed with a determined violence to join the ocean where its aggression would dissipate in the warm embrace of depth and breadth.

His choices were few. He could drop into the water and never be missed, except by his parents. Or he could die of torture, starvation and the diseases of rats and venomous bats in the dungeon. And still not be missed. He mulled over the two choices. He couldn't think clearly. All he could see was her face. He could almost taste her lips. He could almost feel...he could feel how warm she was.

He turned with a start when he heard voices. Soldiers. Infantrymen, from the looks of them, returning from that business in Africa.

Jack forced a smile. "Evenin', gentlemen."

"Evenin' to you, Guv," they said, too drunk to realize his white scarf was not part of a proper suit of gentleman's clothing.

"Say," he asked, "could you lads point me in the right direction if a fellow wanted to sign on to serve Her Majesty's good war in Africa?"

And that's how it ended. Apparently.

ELEVEN

Victoria was restless. As far as her family knew, she had a touch of chest congestion. She was left to her bedroom, and every day became like the one before it. Her meals were brought up on a tray, and each afternoon, her father would come in for a brief visit.

"Well, that's not how it's meant to work," he said one day during the second week of bed rest. "I'm on the mend, and you've just come down with a chest infection! At least it's not your heart," he said with a smile as he took a chair alongside her bed."

"It's not?" she whispered. "Hmmm."

"Of course it's not your heart, darling! You're far too young and in otherwise perfect health. I daresay you're stronger than your brothers in some regards!"

"Where are my brothers?" she asked. "No brother whatsoever on the guest list!"

55

"Ah well, that's part my fault," her father said. "I sent them out to look for your young Jack Pierce."

Victoria coughed, but it almost sounded like a choke.

"Here, dear, have a sip," said her father, handing her a tumbler of water.

"What do you mean 'look for' Jack Pierce?" she asked. "Is he missing?"

"Apparently so," said her father, smoothing out the arms of his jacket. "It took me a while, but I believe I found a position for him over at old Dunleavy's office, sorting through bills of lading, checking on shipments, that kind of thing. I've not forgot that young gentleman. He's bright with a good manner and excellent speech. Could have fooled me that he isn't one of us, actually."

"One of us?"

"Oh, you know, darling, one of our kind. Not peerage, of course, but he certainly sounds as though he could have been raised in a baronetcy. Has he any schooling, do you know?"

"I'm sure I don't know, father," Victoria said quietly. "I know he reads and writes quite handsomely." She looked up to see her father's eyebrows rise in an arch of inquiry. "I saw his chapbook...that first day he brought you home," she said.

Not strictly the truth...but I have seen it.

"Fancies himself some sort of writer I think. Not that I've read any of it."

That part was true. *He never let me read it. Said he might, someday.*

"Well, near as I can determine, he's gone off to Africa. A shame too as that Godforsaken place will be the end of most of the lads!"

"No!" cried Victoria.

"Well, sorry to put it that way, sweet daughter, but that's why I'm keeping my sons, your brothers, from it. Even in a leadership position, it's quite the world's end."

"But Daddy!" Victoria said, covering her personal angst with apparent concern for the world, "I heard you tell Auntie that it was a worthy cause!"

"Yes, well, it's a lost cause, but a worthy one, at that," he mumbled. "As lost causes go, it's quite worthy of being called that!" he added triumphantly.

Victoria grinned. *He didn't even notice my reaction to the news about Jack.* "Somehow I don't believe Auntie thought you meant quite that!"

"No, probably not," he agreed. "Ah, say, do you by any chance remember your cousin Alice?"

"I don't have a cousin Alice, Daddy." Victoria said.

"Yes, right, well, no, she's not really your cousin, but your mother considered her mother Emily to be like a sister. Tight as thieves, those two. Emily's father-in-law is John Ponsonby, 3rd Earl of Westbourne. I received a rather strange note from Emily this morning. Her daughter has gone missing."

"Missing?"

"I don't know how the grand-daughter of an Earl goes missing, especially as she is eventually expected to inherit the baronetcy as Countess of Westbourne, but apparently she's not been seen for nearly a month. Now, mind you, she stays in London with another family, friends of Lord Ponsonby, but they've not seen her either. Bit of an artist type. Allright, they called her bohemian, but I'm sure that's not the case, despite Emily and Edward's rather willful elopement and unconventional life. Still, the young lady is missing."

"Ah, yes, mummy's friend Auntie Emily, who was not

actually my aunt. But Alice? I thought they had a little boy. I don't remember Alice."

"Well, anyway, I'm off to the Ponsonbys for a long, arduous dinner. You rest now."

"Yes, Daddy, I will," she said, slipping down under her sheet. "Why arduous?"

"Because Emily was really your mother's friend, and I've never quite got the essence of Edward. Oh, he'll be the next Earl of Westbourne, no doubt of it, but for now, he's a painter—quite good from what I understand. But, he mumbles. And I've no idea about what. I warrant I'll have to listen to how the Ponsonbys had hoped their only daughter would marry your eldest brother, who, coincidently, is rather taken by that lovely Lady Mary Wellington. On the other hand, perhaps they won't."

"Really!" exclaimed Victoria. "I had no idea my brother was interested in a member of the Wellington family."

"Only the prettiest one," he assured her, as he bent down to kiss her cheek. "I know Emily and Edward will want me to help them find Alice, though I've not got a clue where to begin." He reached for the doorknob and paused.

"Daddy, didn't my real Auntie call Mummy a bohemian?"

"Why, how queer that you've recalled that! Yes, she did. We considered it quite the compliment! I'm off now. Rest well, sweet daughter."

"Thank you, Daddy, I shall." *I shall not!*

As soon as her father had closed the door to her suite, Victoria leaped out of bed and moved quickly to the corner of the room where the world globe was stationed on a lovely brass stand.

Oh my, that is the world's end. It will take me months

and months to get there. Damn it, Jack! You will NOT get away with this!

TWELVE

Victoria Dormier knew when she awakened from her fainting spell that she was falling in love with a woman. That's what made her faint.

Everyone at home was all tut-tut and "poor thing" and "must have caught a bug," but Victoria knew otherwise. Jack Pierce was a bug, true, but he was no...he was not a he. He was a she. And she was a bug, and Victoria aimed to squash her. Oh sure, Victoria loved Jack, she was sure of that. So what? He...she...had lied. He was...she was the very meaning of deception. Jack...good Lord! What was Jack's real name, then?

She sat down hard. She looked out her window at something that may as well have been nothing because her vision was blurred with her tears. The only thing worse than discovering Jack was a woman, which in and of itself was not so terrible, truth be told, was the realization that she had no one to talk to about this. No confidant. No trusted best friend. No one who would have the slightest idea on earth what she was talking about. No one. Not even Alexis.

Lord! Alexis would be mortified!

A knock at the door brought her out of her fog. The houseman announced the arrival of Her Majesty's courier, which turned out to be none other than her Private Secretary, Benson, who walked right through the doorway without being asked. He looked around the small suite, sniffed and strode toward her.

"A message from Her Majesty."

"Hello to you, too, Benson. May I offer you tea?"

"I think not," he answered.

Victoria reached for the envelope and looked at the handwriting. Benson stood with his hands behind his back.

"I'm to await an answer by return," he said when Victoria frowned up at him.

She scanned the note quickly. She sighed. She read it again. She sighed again.

"Benson, how did you happen to be right where I was with the carriage the night I fainted?"

"In Jack Pierce's arms?" Benson asked. "A friend who was under the weather asked me to fill in for him, and as it was my night off, it seemed something a friend would do. Pure happenstance, my lady."

Victoria snorted. *Oh, right, and you think you are such a gentleman, said no one ever!*

"Please tell Her Majesty I will arrive at the appointed time," she said aloud.

"That would be in three hours, then," announced Benson.

Victoria sighed. "Yes, Benson, I know what time it is.

Thank you. That will be all."

He turned to leave, then paused. "You'll dress for dinner, then?" he asked, looking at her clothing.

An assortment of inappropriate quips went through her mind. She settled on a sweet smile and "Of course, Benson," which had the desired effect of him leaving immediately.

"No, I thought I'd just show up in my pink pyjamas and robe," she snarled after the door closed. "Oh dash! Dash, dash, dash, bloody dash!"

***

For the first half of the meal, Queen Victoria said nothing. She made a few noises as she slurped her soup, scraped her plate and rang her bell, but she said nothing to her niece. They were dining alone. Finally, as the Queen mopped up some remaining gravy from her plate with a piece of soft French bread, she spoke.

"In the first place, niece, I know you smoke as I can smell it."

Victoria forgot she had a tin of cigarettes in her bag that she had been carrying to give to Jack next time she saw him. *The bug.*

"Would you like one, Auntie?"

"I think so, but let's go into the library and stand outside the French doors so no one can see us. Well, we'll have my man Arthur, but he won't say a word."

The Queen squinted, her failing eyesight failing her more. "In the second place, we are not fond of that head ornament."

"Head orn—oh!"

"We fail to see the charm in something so black.

Unless one is in mourning."

Victoria ran her fingers through her mop of hair. The spikes were gone, but the color remained. "I'm throwing it away when I get home," she said. "A bit chilly this evening, Auntie."

"Is this not what shawls are for, niece? Come."

The Queen rose from the table with the help of her footman but waved him away, and she and her niece walked toward the library. Arthur busied himself lighting a fire, putting up a few candles, re-arranging the cushions on the sofa. Overall, it was a cozy room darkened by shadows from ceiling-high bookshelves that no one could possibly reach and drenched in more hunting scenes on toile than any monarch had a right to like. The Queen opened the French doors herself, wrapped the shawl around her shoulders and asked her niece for a light.

"This did not take place," the Queen said.

"No, no it didn't," answered Victoria.

"Well, aren't you going to have one?"

"I actually don't smoke, Auntie...these were for...a friend."

"And that would be your friend Jack Pierce, am I correct? I know I am. Jack. Odd name for a woman, is it not?"

"Oh, I think it's short for something," Victoria said. "What a gorgeous sky tonight! Clear with stars." *How does she know about Jack?*

"And what is your relationship with 'Jack' niece? Do we know her family?"

"I don't believe you do, Auntie—I don't think Jack has a family."

Her?Did she just say 'her'?

"Oh, pshaw, niece! Everyone has a family! Some are

just better at hiding it than others."

"Perhaps," Victoria sighed. "Well, anyway, I don't expect to remain friends with Jack."

The Queen puffed on her cigarette. Big inhale, big exhale. Victoria continued her intense fascination with the sky.

"Oh, have you had a falling out with your Jack, already?"

"Not my Jack," Victoria whispered.

"Hmm."

"Can we go inside, Auntie? I'm quite chilled, and I really ought to be starting for home soon. You need your rest."

They went inside, but the Queen motioned her niece to be seated. She had Arthur stir the fire up a bit, poured herself a good-sized brandy, then plopped into her over-stuffed chair.

"Tell your auntie what the trouble is, won't you? I know you, niece. You are troubled."

Victoria Dormier stared into the fire. The heat failed to keep her eyes from becoming damp. She didn't let a tear fall, but she knew if she blinked it would.

"Are you in love with Jack, dear niece?"

Victoria blinked.

"I thought so," the Queen said. "I know the signs. I shall never forget when my beloved, darling Bertie had to return home after we first met. I was forlorn. But he came back. And I asked him to marry me!"

"Oh Auntie, I can't marry Jack! You know I cannot!" Victoria wiped her cheek with her little finger as if using the small one would make the event small.

"Actually, you can marry Jack. It's what'shername you cannot marry."

"Who is 'what'shername'?"

"What'shername! Jack! You know...Alice. Alice Ponsonby. I suppose Jack is short for Alice, then. Your mother was her mother's Bestie."

"Her what?" asked Victoria.

"Her Bestie, her best friend. I never approved, but there you have it. Anyway, as long as she is Jack, I do believe you can marry."

Victoria Dormier looked at her aunt, the Queen of England. *Is the old bird inebriated?*

"Are you quite four sheets to the wind, Auntie?"

"Wouldn't you be if you just found out your favorite niece was a Sappho?"

"I suppose so, Auntie, but I'm too upset to think. I loved her when I thought she was Jack, and now that I know Jack is not a he, I find I'm no less in love. I am so confused, and now it doesn't matter as he's...she's gone off to Africa to fight that war of yours and will no doubt be killed!"

"What war? Oh, that little skirmish? I'd hardly call it a war."

"Well, everyone else does!"

"Do they now? I'll look into it. But back to Jack...actually, there is something even more important I wanted to ask."

"Something more important than Jack?"

"Don't look so surprised, niece! Yes, but perhaps it is, or could be, distantly relevant to Jack, too. What is this Magick I've heard you engage in?"

Victoria's eyes widened. "Daddy said you didn't believe in it!"

"Oh, Daddy can go to hell," the Queen shot back. "And I can say that since he's my half-brother. He hasn't a clue what I do or don't believe in." She reached for her brandy snifter.

"I think Daddy's ill...I mean, seriously ill, Auntie."

The Queen stopped her arm mid-drink. She replaced the crystal on the side table. "Can you help him? With your Magick?"

"He says it's too far gone. He...well, Auntie, he says I'm to save it."

"What in God's name would you be saving it for, your old age? Don't bother. It's a maddening condition, at best, old age. But incurable, so perhaps my brother knows whereof he speaks."

The Queen glanced at her niece while pretending not to. She worked her mouth into a suitable twist and said, "Come here, darling. Come sit with your Auntie."

Victoria Dormier slid off the sofa and sat upon a cushion on the floor next to the Queen's chair. She felt her auntie rubbing her head, and clucking softly about love. Sometimes, Auntie said, you have to go where love takes you. Victoria realized that her Auntie knew many things about the subject.

"I want to go to Africa," announced Victoria. "I can shoot."

"So can I," said the Queen, "but I don't expect to go to Africa to do it. Plenty of fowl right here. Not that I've been riding, of late."

"Auntie, could I not join the Army Nursing Service? They'd let me in on your command."

"Niece, the sight of blood makes you faint. You've been that way since you were a wee child."

Victoria thought about it for a moment. "I've learnt how to drive a motorbike, Auntie! My brother showed me how when he got his Singer!"

"I should report him to the authorities," the Queen said.

Victoria giggled. "Oh Auntie, you *are* the authorities! But don't you see? I could be a driver. They need drivers in the Army Nursing Service."

"I know all about it," the Queen assured her. "I've arranged through my dear grandson Willy to have two dozen early production pieces shipped to Africa from Nuremberg. He could hardly turn down his granny! They arrived a month or so ago. Noisy contraptions from what I understand. By this time next year they'll go into full production and be everywhere, Willy says."

"That's wonderful!" Victoria jumped up.

"Niece, please. I cannot tolerate noise the way I used to."

"Oh sorry, Auntie, I just got overstimulated! But would you? Would you consider getting someone to allow me in?"

Queen Victoria looked to her left. "Arthur?"

"Ma'am?"

"Get Benson for me first thing in the morning."

Arthur inclined his head. "Ma'am."

Victoria Dormier sat back down on the floor and leaned up against her auntie's chair. The Queen sloughed off her slippers.

"Can I rub them for you, Auntie?" Victoria asked but didn't wait for an answer. She began rubbing the chubby little feet before the Queen could object.

From the murmurs of pleasure, she knew her auntie was enjoying the foot massage. "I'm not all that well myself," she said to her niece.

Victoria Dormier said nothing. She sensed as much when she saw how puffy and pale her Auntie seemed during dinner. Of course, some of that was the dinner.

"So I need you to take care of yourself," the Queen said. "I do have questions about this African situation. I'm hearing contradictory reports."

"Yes, Auntie. I will be honored and pleased to provide you with a full report. When might I leave for Africa, then?"

"And what of my brother? Will he allow it?" She peered at her niece over her eyeglasses. "Not that I have to ask him," she mumbled.

"He would forbid me to stay here and mope!"

Abruptly the Queen scooted forward in her chair. "I'm to bed now, niece." Even with her niece helping her, it was a struggle to get her out of the chair. Arthur quietly assisted.

"I'll have Benson come 'round with my *letter close* tomorrow. I can't imagine anyone will find fault with it. Go see my dear daughter Lenchen, your cousin. She'll take care of the particulars, and she'll be discreet. She's quite aware of the situation down in Africa as my grandson Christie serves there under General Sir Redvers Buller. We've understood it's a smallish local thing. Christie is quite a good soldier I'm told." The Queen gazed off into the distance. "He was a lovely child and still quite my favorite grandchild."

Victoria had met her second cousin once, but barely remembered what he looked like.

The Queen turned to leave the room. "Keep this all confidential—no one should know you are in Africa lest you become a target for either the enemy or...anyone. Even Christie has Buller and Baden-Powell looking after him. And don't stay long. And bring Jack back. Jack was my secret weapon."

Victoria let go of the Queen's arm. "What do you mean, 'your secret weapon,' Auntie?"

The Queen looked down at her arm as if it were an unwelcome appendage. After a beat, she used it to pat Victoria's arm. "A Queen without a secret is like a...samurai without a sword!

"One should always have some secrets, niece. I've not actually met Jack, but she serves in my intelligence corp. All very hush-hush, you know. I was against it until her grandfather asked a special favor of me. It seems Jack, like her mother, has always had a bit of the bohemian in her. We've merely put it to good use. She's out and about with the beastie boys, and I'm not told the particulars for fear I'd collapse at the unsavoriness of it."

Victoria Dormier's mouth was open, and her eyes were wide with alarm. Besties and beasties? Bohemian? Buller? Baden-Powell. This evening was becoming an alliterative nightmare from whence Victoria feared she would not awaken.

"Oh niece, don't look so shocked. It's 1900 for heaven's sake. Turn of the century, wave of the future and all that other mischief. But, that's the way is it. Besides, generally speaking, I believe Jack will, ultimately, keep my sweet niece out of trouble, and I approve of the match."

The match? What match? I'm planning to murder Jack when next I see her!

"Go on, now, be a good niece and go see about that situation down in Africa. And don't stay longer than one month."

"Will that be quite enough time, Auntie, to investigate for you?"

"It will have to be. I'm simply not feeling all that well, and I want to wrap up a few loose ends. This Africa conflict is one. Goodnight, niece, be good."

She walked several steps then stopped and turned. "Never mind the part about being good, niece! Carry on as you are—it's been marvelous and refreshing for an old woman to see such enthusiasm for life. I share it not, but I know it when I see it. And remember—the smoking part? It did not occur."

Victoria gave a deep and formal curtsey. "Never happened, Your Grace." she whispered. Her mind was firing blanks: *Secret weapon? Keep me out of trouble! Ha!* Victoria had a lot of questions, but the Queen was done.

She watched as the old lady's bustle swung behind her like...like an extra behind. She silently giggled at the concept and peered after Queen Victoria as she slowly made her way down the long hallway. Apparently she knew her niece's gaze followed her because just before she turned the corner, she raised her left hand in a backwards wave.

Two weeks later, Victoria Dormier spoke to her cousin Lenchen. As the third daughter and fifth child of the Queen and Prince Albert, Princess Helena Augusta Victoria was a formidable presence to most, but to Dormier, she was a pussycat compared to her mother, the Queen. Arrangements were made for Dormier to be on limited assignment as a Driver, Army Nursing Service.

Unfortunately, Daddy died suddenly, and Victoria lost all desire to do anything. Including search for Jack...or Alice. She thought about Jack, but every time she did, she had to think about Alice. She decided to stop thinking of either...well...not often anyway.

THIRTEEN

As the days became weeks, Victoria's brothers tried everything to ease her grief. Nothing was working. Finally, her sister, Alexis, suggested they visit their father's grave. To the average 18-year old, it might not sound like a pleasant way to spend the morning, but to Victoria it had a timely appeal. She was depressed, and she was a bit gothic in her tastes. A cemetery seemed just the thing!

Once there, they placed a bouquet of fresh flowers at the foot of the family crypt.

"They're both here," Victoria whispered. "Mummy and Daddy...ohhhhh...." She began to weep, then sob, then shiver.

Alexis frowned. "Well, we'll all be here sooner or later, and at least they're together."

Victoria's eyes crossed. "I shan't end up here," she protested. "I shall be buried with my beloved."

"And who might that be, dearest sister?" She put her arm around her sister's shoulder and pulled her in close. "I'm hearing rumors," Alexis said. She dropped down onto the soft grass under the shade of an ancient oak tree and extended a hand to her sister.

"Impossible! I've been nowhere in weeks!"

"These are old rumors," Alexis said, poking at errant blades of grass.

Dormier looked at her in alarm but said nothing. Finally: "From whence did you hear such contrivances?"

Alexis looked at her and smiled. She hesitated. "From...from Daddy, sweetheart. He thought you might be sweet on someone."

"Who, pray tell!"

"Do you remember cousin Alice?"

Dormier turned to her. "Alex, we don't have a cousin Alice! Daddy asked me the same question months ago. Alice was mummy's best friend's daughter, and not really our cousin."

Alexis remained silent. She absently brushed some dried petals off the surface of the marble surround.

"That's true," Alexis said finally. "She wasn't our cousin. And she wasn't known as Alice the last few years, either."

Victoria glanced at her sister. *What does she know?* "Look at that," she cried. "Our cousin Mary's marker!" She pointed to an adjacent headstone.

"Father said you were falling for Alice Ponsonby," she blurted out, her cheeks coloring as she said it.

"I don't even know Alice Ponsonby, Alexis! I met her once, maybe twice, and furthermore...furthermore..." Victoria looked around wildly for something to focus on instead of her sister. "Furthermore," she continued after a moment, "Furthermore—

"Oh Victoria, it's quite all right, darling. Don't be ashamed or shy. Daddy was quite pleased that you might have found someone to love."

"He was?"

"Of course he was. As am I," she added.

Dormier saw the blush in her sister's cheeks and reached for her. "Oh, Alex, how could I not have known that you'd love me no less? And, and it's true, I guess."

"You guess, sister?"

"Well, yes, I mean, it's true but I thought Alice was Jack."

"For how long? An hour?" teased Alex.

It was Dormier's turn to blush. "Well...I knew something was different. Off really. I knew, but I didn't recognize him as Alice Ponsonby! Oh dash, Alex, I knew something, somewhere in my heart of hearts! And right away, yes, I concede. He seemed familiar. 'Twas Auntie who let the kitty out of the bag."

"I declare: That is a surprise!"

"I thought so, too," Dormier mumbled.

They walked back down the hill and into the waiting carriage. "Will you go to Africa, now, sister?"

Victoria thought about the question. *I'd like to kick his shins as soon as possible.* "Yes," she answered. "How soon do you think we might have my trunks brought 'round and packed?"

Alexis laughed. "I rather doubt you'll be wanting trunks, darling. A large rucksack perhaps. It's a war in Africa you're going to Victoria, not a regatta at the Isle of Wight."

They walked back to their house, pausing several times to admire a stranger's garden.

"Hmm," murmured Alexis. "There is something that rather worries me, though. When have you ever known our royal relative to be so agreeable?"

Victoria looked hard at her sister. "Well, the old girl's off her stride, you know. Doesn't look well. But, you're right: Never! Should I be suspicious?"

"Only if you know her!" They giggled walking home arm-in-arm.

"And you'll never guess! She even asked me about...you know, the hocus pocus."

Alexis nodded. "She's definitely up to something."

"Well, good Lord! How am I to know what it is?"

Alexis shook her head. "I'd go with what Daddy always said when his sister confounded him. 'You'll know it when you see it, and duck before it kills you!'"

***

The Empress of practically the whole world decided not to let on that she knew exactly where Jack was. It didn't matter: Jack wouldn't be in that Godforsaken continent for long. She wouldn't be there at all if her niece had the slightest instinct for determining the difference between a male and a female. Never mind. They'd both be back within a few weeks.

Queen Victoria gave a little laugh. She had her own suspicions about these continuing assassination rumors, but she needed facts. The wrong words in the right ear would tell her much of what she needed to know. She thought they were scare tactics more than anything.

Why kill me, I've got one foot in the grave as it is!

But if it turned out to be more, then Jack could take care of the details upon her return.

Assuming I don't get myself blown away in the next month, this whole Jack and Victoria in Africa thing could be the perfect foil for a little behind-the-scenes investigating myself.

"Never assume," she said aloud to no one.

"I beg pardon, Ma'am?" Benson stepped from the shadows.

"Benson, don't hover! You gave me a fright. And what are you doing here?"

"Sorry, Ma'am," he said. "I've brought correspondence for your signature." His eyes narrowed as she waved him away. Then, "Well what am I signing? Let's get on with it."

"The usual, Ma'am, mostly sending regrets to events you cannot attend."

"Will not attend," she corrected.

"Yes, Ma'am. And the *letters close*, including one for that...for your niece, Ma'am. To be a driver, I believe, Ma'am." He sniffed, audibly.

Queen Victoria gave Benson a sidelong glance as he bent over the various piece of paper. "Ah yes, well I think it's good that my niece is off to Africa to see what's really going on there."

Benson was handing her the pen but stopped mid-gesture. "Africa! Quite a danger down there, Ma'am, for a young lady."

"Yes, but she'll be watched over by an officer, some fellow named Pierce, friend of the family I suppose. He'll look after her. He knows who he'll have to answer to if not!"

Benson's back was now to the Queen, but she noted his posture relaxed. He turned and nodded. "Yes, Ma'am, I rather expect he does." *It's the best place for them*, he said under his breath.

When Benson left, Arthur entered with tea service. He placed it near her favorite chair, and then gave her his arm as they walked to it.

"May I pour, Ma'am?"

"Yes, Arthur, do. Say! What do you think of Benson, Arthur?"

Arthur stood up straight. "I never think of him, Ma'am. Will that be all, Ma'am?"

She waved him away, took a sip of her tea and smiled. Arthur loathes Benson. That is what she would have guessed. Arthur had been with her for 47 years, or was it 48? She yawned. She was tired. Tired as faded velvet. Eighty years old, weary, tired. But she had one last goal to accomplish. Her grandson, Kaiser Wilhelm of Germany, was not going to wage a war during her lifetime. No, he was not! If she had to use her niece to deliver that message to convince dear Willy, then so be it. And if the Queen of England had to enlist the help of her darling bohemian niece's boy/girl heartthrob, well...the Queen of England knew all about true love. Oh, yes she did!

FOURTEEN

The trip to The Cape Colony took 19 days, two days longer than usual. Victoria mentally calculated that Jack was nearly two months ahead of her. As a driver messenger between the base and field hospitals and the men on the front line, Victoria's job was to assess the number of front line wounded soldiers the field hospital could expect to receive on any given day of actual fighting. The field hospitals were set up two to three miles from the front lines, well behind the fire-power danger zone. Still, the camp guards stayed on high alert during actual fighting to avoid the ever-present danger of the enemy flanking the British and coming up unannounced into the lap of hospital and medic personnel; it had happened numerous times.

Victoria chided herself for not being more specific when she asked Lenchen to locate which regiment Jack had joined. Her Highness had narrowed it down to one of two regiments. Actually she got her information from her mother, the Queen. Dormier stirred in her cot. It was certainly handy to have the Queen of England as one's auntie, but someone ought to have a word with Her Highness about the bedding. On the other hand, she was allowed to wear khaki trousers like the Nursing officers instead of long gowns, aprons and caps like the actual nurses. No one called her Sister and though her rank was a mere private, she was allowed to carry a sidearm. She'd have to remember to review how to use it. With that thought, Victoria fell sound asleep.

Two hours later, she was unceremoniously awakened by reveille. She leapt off her cot, ran to the privy, splashed water on her face and was in uniform within 15 minutes. As she stood with the others outside the canteen, sipping coffee and waiting for their turn to go into the mess tent and eat some breakfast, Capt. Rosemary Privet strode up to her. Victoria dropped the tin cup and saluted.

"Private, I want you to take this message to Captain Hardinage on the front line, and if you can't locate him, give it to Lieutenant Pierce or whoever's officer in command. And since you'll probably die doing it, I guess this is goodbye, then."

"Yes, ma'am." *Lieutenant Pierce?*

"'Yes, ma'am' what, Private?"

"Yes, ma'am. Thank you ma'am. Goodbye ma'am."

"That's better, Private. Now go!"

Captain Privet kept her smile to herself as the citizen-soldier gunned her motorcycle. They were brave, these drivers, and this one was pretty. Terrible to waste lives like this. The Boers seemed determined to take their land back by force, and the Germans, safe in Germany, were always on the sidelines urging the Boer troops on with bits of intelligence, some weaponry and a great deal of encouragement.

Captain Privet saluted a few soldiers who passed her carrying an empty litter. The morgue would be filling up within hours. Soon the ambulance drivers would have to stack the bodies inside their lorries and make a run for it behind the lines. Some might not make it. A wayward cannon ball. A lucky sniper. Any number of things could keep the living from carting the dead to a proper burial. It had happened. A couple of snappy drivers, a truck full of corpses, and without warning, the drivers were dead and the dead were as good as twice dead. But the drivers! Young, all of them. All dedicated, full of courage, full of fear. Doing it anyway. Driving the dead. Dying for the dead.

Privet hopped up the three steps to the officers' tent. Inside, Jones was sleeping or trying to. Montgomery was reading. St. James was buffing her toes. All four of them were officers, with Privet the senior.

"Did you send Private Dormier off with your usual farewell," asked St. James. She looked up at Privet under her long, dark blonde hair

"Of course."

"Why do you do that? You know it makes the riders more nervous than they already are."

Jones stirred in her bed and covered her head. "Why do you talk so loudly, St. Bitch?" she mumbled.

St. James raised her index finger in the direction of the mound of blankets.

"Because," answered Privet, looking at the formless heap of army blankets covering Jones, "we really don't know if they're going to make it. Or come back."

"We've lost exactly one rider to the front in a year," said St. James.

Juliet Montgomery put her book down and stared vacantly at Privet. Privet saw the movement out of the corner of her eye.

"Don't worry, Julie," she said, "St. James is just trying to toughen me up."

Montgomery opened her mouth to speak, then closed it. Then she swallowed hard. "Still," she said softly, "it must hurt awfully much, even after all this time." She glanced at St. James, who continued working on her toes, head down.

Privet gave Montgomery a quick smile. 'Thank you,' she mouthed silently. As Privet turned toward her bunk, a huge explosion from the direction of the front, a quarter mile away rocked the wooden foundation of their tent. Jones jumped out of bed fully clothed and grabbed her helmet. St. James and Montgomery did the same. Privet froze. As the others ran out of the tent and down the stairs, the smell of gunpowder filled the air. Privet made the sign of the cross and turned to exit the tent. Another pretty one gone. Another letter home to stunned parents. The only problem was, Privet didn't know her first name.

***

Victoria adjusted her goggles, leaned low on her seat and gunned the motorcycle up a small hill. Once there, she could see the layout of the entire valley. The Boers were flanked to her left and around an elbow of small earthen mounds to the right. She had to roll silently down the steep incline, staying close to the edge of the road in the hopes that the sickly grove of beat up poplars would help hide her. Once at the bottom of the incline, she'd have to traverse a narrow gully that would take her up behind a large hill on her left and to the Allies front line command post. That would be the dangerous part. *Could it be? Could she be delivering a message to Lt. Jack Pierce? Her Jack Pierce? Oh, this would be special.*

'Oh, hello Jack, fancy meeting you here, in Africa, in a war. No, you didn't say goodbye, did you? By the time I noticed, you were probably already here.'

From the gully, she'd have to gun the motor bike up another incline, the one that could be clearly seen from the enemy outposts behind the small mounds to her left. She'd done this trip a week earlier, but that was before the Boers wound their way around to the left, essentially creating a block that would soon place them between the Allies' front line and the nurses' encampment. Privet had told everyone they were moving the main camp a mile to the east to be a good mile directly behind their troops, but it hadn't happened yet. *Privet.*

Holy hell! So this is goodbye? I don't think so. I don't damn think so.

Victoria looked around before beginning her silent descent. To her left, the Allies were safely behind two major hills and behind that another, higher hill. As Victoria watched the smoke from the cannon volleys, she saw that all of the shots hit right below the hill in front of the line. None of the canons seemed to be in striking distance of the trenches just over the crest of the Allies' hills. She wondered if the slow Boer encroachment to the right, behind the smaller mounds, was a prelude to setting up canons that would crest the Allies' two hills and cause a frightful amount of damage. Had anyone actually looked at this layout from the perspective she had right then?

As she mentally prepared herself for the descent, the sun glanced off something in the sky and shot a stream of intense light onto the ground right in front of her. Laying her bike down, she crawled into the bushes to the side of the road, and that's when she saw it. A dirigible was approaching the Allies' front line from behind. Victoria saw a single Iron Cross, like that of the Reichskriegsflagge, emblazoned on its side. The British troops hadn't seen it. They couldn't see it. Suddenly the volleys from the Boer side increased in frequency. They were too far away for accuracy, but the noise and smoke alone was frightening. They had seen the airship creeping silently up behind their enemy.

It's a distraction! They don't want anyone to turn around and look up.

Victoria had no way of knowing for sure if the airship was armed, but she could take no chances.

Oh Jack, for God's sake, look up!

Victoria reached inside her leather jacket and felt in her interior pocket for her leather case. She opened it slowly and took out the mirrors.

Would there be time?

Quickly she set up one mirror to capture the German airship. Then she attached another mirror to it at a forty-five degree angle.

The most she could hope for was that she could send the hologram so close to the Allies' front line that they would have to turn around and look up. Her timing had to be perfect. Her hands shook with the adrenalin rush of knowing she was the only person on earth who might be able to save the Allies' front line. The downside was that the mirrors would give away her position. She knelt on the ground and secured the mirrors, then picked up her bike and turned it back in the direction of her camp. Once the hologram had been seen by the Boers, she'd have to get down off her hill quickly. Unlike her own side's front line, she was in range of the snipers if not the cannon volleys.

As she aimed the first mirror at the dirigible, she moved the holographic image that resulted from the second mirror as close to the front line as she could.

Look up, damn it, look up!

Maybe it was someone lying on his back. Maybe it was someone daydreaming about home. Whoever saw the hologram started firing, and then suddenly the Allies' cannons were turned around and pointing up into the sky. In a second, they'd see the actual airship. With the split-second timing of pure luck, as she had zero experience, she closed down the hologram. She thought she had seen a rip in the skin of the actual airship caused by the intense heat from her reflective mirror. She placed the mirrors back into their case and crawled over to her bike. She jumped on it and stepped on the gas pedal. As she throttled forward, a searing pain ripped through her right shoulder and a massive explosion shook the airwaves in all directions. She held onto the bike with her left hand and made it halfway down the hill when the loss of blood, the pain and the fear threw her into a state of shock.

She yelled as loudly as she could. "Holy bloody hell— you don't deserve this, Jack Pierce! I could have you court marshalled! I am not going to die for you, and—"

The bike went down, landing on her left leg, and the last thing she remembered was the echo of the Allied troops shouting a huge hurrah.

****

FIFTEEN

Every driver started her engine. Nurses and medics were scrambling for seats in the back of the ambulances, medical bags on their laps, helmets on their heads and a breathy fear in their whispered voices.

"Five coaches in each contingent!" Second Lt. Agnes Jones yelled loudly to the nurses milling around. "Make six groups of five, and plan to leave in five-minute increments."

Thirty ambulances, fashioned basically from truck lorries, rolled into a rough configuration of six groups. Jones was in charge of the drive to the front, with Montgomery organizing the two tent hospitals, each capable of holding about thirty beds.

Privet stepped out of the officers' tent and waved away the dust kicked up by the running feet and moving tires. "Hold on, Lieutenant," she shouted. "Let's send a couple cyclists up to see what we're in for."

"I'd say we're in for hell," yelled Jones, unable to hide her look of disbelief at the delay.

"True enough," agreed Privet. "Let's just see whose hell it is." She motioned to a couple motorcyclists who were sitting astride their bikes ready to go. "Soldiers! Head on up that hill where the messenger went, and see what you can see. Ought to take ten minutes up and back." She looked at her watch and waved them forward.

Everyone watched the two cyclists until they were out of sight. Jones gave the order to turn off the ambulance engines. "Turn 'em off ladies, save the petrol."

Privet walked over toward the nearest hospital tent, where Montgomery was.

"Notice anything funny, Monty?"

"Only that it just became awfully quiet."

"Exactly. Where's the firepower we've heard all morning?"

"What do you think? Is the enemy creeping up on us as we speak?"

"Hope to hell not," said Privet. She reached in her jacket and pulled out a pack of cigarettes. She pumped the pack and held it out to Montgomery.

"Thanks, think I will."

Privet lit both their cigarettes and noticed how Juliet Montgomery's hand shook as she cupped the flame. Privet lit her own and looked around the camp. There was an eerie stillness. Montgomery took several deep drags of her cigarette, then threw it to the ground and snuffed it out with her boot. "Things'll kill you, Privet."

"Something's bound to," she said quietly, enjoying another puff. She blew the smoke out slowly and let it lie languidly in the air between them. "Say, Monty, want to join up for a lovely candle-lit dinner in the canteen tonight?"

Montgomery looked at her. Privet noticed a wry smile creeping across her face. "You're just trying to get my mind off the blood and guts I'm mentally preparing myself to be tending to this evening," said Montgomery.

"Is that a 'No'? Damn."

"Was it really an invitation, Privet?"

"'Rosie, or, if you're feeling formal, 'Rosemary,'" said Privet.

"I like both."

"Yes, actually, it was an invitation," Privet said, snuffing out her cigarette at the sounds of the returning motorcycle. "Hell! Where's the second rider?"

She walked briskly to the front of the ambulance line where the rider was gesturing towards the direction from where she had come. St. James was listening to the rider and looked back to see Privet just as she approached.

"Dormier's down," said St. James. "Second driver stayed with her. We need to send an ambulance up. Sounds like she got shot returning here."

"Doesn't seem she's been gone long enough to have delivered the message to Lieutenant Pierce," said Privet.

"Doesn't, does it?" said St. James.

Privet looked up the hill. "Allright, then, let's get Dormier back here. Better take the rider so she can drive Dormier's bike back."

Before the ambulance was out of sight, Privet saw two male soldiers running down the long hill toward the camp. She knew they were Allied troops because the ambulance didn't slow down as it came upon them.

She walked toward the front of the ambulance brigade to greet the envoy.

"Captain!" the two soldiers saluted as they slowed.

They were out of breath and red-faced.

"What's going on up there, soldiers?" asked Privet.

"Somebody just shot the hell out of a German dirigible," said one.

"Yeah, thing went up in flames. And Captain, wasn't any of us that shot it. Hell we didn't even see it creeping up behind us."

"Them," the other man said. "There were two of 'em, Captain."

"Two?" she said. "They both got shot down?"

"Well, that's the strange thing. One caught on fire and crashed and the other just disappeared."

"Into thin air," the first soldier said. He was almost whispering. "Like it wasn't even there!"

"What did the Boer lines do?" she asked.

"They started running," one soldier said. "They broke up their front lines and backed way up. At least a half mile."

"Huh," mumbled Privet. "That doesn't make a lot of sense. They'd be backed up to the river. Unless they plan to cross it and lose their front lines all the way."

"Captain," said one of the soldiers, "Lieutenant Pierce told us to tell you it's safe to move your encampment back behind our lines now."

"Good," said Privet. "We don't much like being flanked by both friend and foe with nothing in front of us but open territory. You men rest a bit, get some grub and water, and tell Lieutenant Pierce we'll be moving out tonight under cover of darkness. Tell him we'll set up about a quarter mile behind his last trenches. I'll give you a note for him—I could use some help with the move."

"Yes ma'am, thank you ma'am."

Privet looked off into the distance where the blast had

occurred. The blue sky revealed nothing. She walked back to the infirmary and lifted the tent flap. She saw Montgomery scrubbing up, two nurses alongside her doing the same. "Date's off, Monty," she called out. "Right after you finish fixing up Dormier, we're packing up to move behind the lines. Looks like the Boers saw their ally's flying cigar blow up and took off running."

Montgomery turned slightly and grinned. "I knew you were all talk, Rosemary."

Privet smiled. "Not quite. I'm rain-checking that dinner."

With that, she dropped the tent flap and walked away. She'd heard vague references to someone back home, but she didn't know and didn't really want to know the details. She knew the good doctor was teasing her, playing along. Trouble was, Privet wished Montgomery wasn't teasing. She wished Montgomery were as available as she was accepting. But she had a talk with herself. *Watch it, Privet. The woman likes you, as a friend. She knows what you like, and she likes you anyway. Don't mess it up.*

****

SIXTEEN

Private Dormier had a fever-driven delirium that Montgomery had seen too many times. The bullet, now removed, had gone deep. But no major arteries had been damaged, no bone fragments had splintered into tissue, killing muscle, and the infection, kept spotlessly clean by the nurses, would clear up soon. Monty looked at the bullet in the pan. "Looks like a sharpshooter got her. Wonder how far away he was?"

"Close enough to hit his target," mumbled one of the nurses.

"But not close enough to kill her," said Monty. "Or maybe he wasn't trying to kill her."

"That would be a first," said the nurse.

"I know. It's curious. This bullet should have killed her or at least caused a lot more damage. It stuck right under her rotator cup. She's sure gonna be sore for a few weeks."

Victoria weaved in and out of consciousness. "Sorry, Auntie."

Monty looked at the nurse.

"Sorry, Auntie," Victoria repeated.

"Nurse Dorothea? When we're done here, will you ask Privet to look up her record? We'll want to advise her parents."

"Get your bloody royal ass over here!" Victoria cried out.

"You a Royal now, are ya?" Dorothea said to Montgomery.

Monty smiled. "Not even distantly related," she said. "Give her another shot of morphine in ten minutes."

After the second shot, Victoria went into a deeper sleep. Within the nether land of memory, imagination and metaphor, the dreams came to life, dreams now distorted by the opiate...her aunt, Queen Victoria had called for her. Again. Apparently, she was in trouble. Again. She looked at her father, who smiled benignly.

"Positive, Victoria. It passes mainly to women through women. We've had one instance of a male having the gift, but that was nine decades ago. But your mother's grandmother, your great-grandmother, was my half-sister Victoria's, eh, Queen Victoria's, aunt. Auntie Adelaide, who was Queen Adelaide."

Victoria's eyes began to cross as she mentally followed the lineage.

"Yes, well, it's a bit complicated because Royals always are, you see. Basically, your mum and your Auntie Victoria, the Queen, had an aunt in common. That would be Addy. She had no children of her own, but she taught the gift to another of her nieces, my beloved Elizabeth, your mother. She felt your mother had the empathetic capacity to absorb most, if not all, of the gift from her. It's pure happenstance that something from my side of the family crossed bloodlines and got passed down to your mother's side and then, of course, to you. And hopefully to a child of yours...or..." he trailed off. Victoria raised an eyebrow but decided to pursue a different path.

"And why didn't Great Grandmother teach it to Auntie?" asked Victoria.

"My sister, well, half-sister, the Queen," he said, "didn't believe in things like the gift. She called it hocus-pocus. I think it frightened her."

"What is it properly called, Daddy?" asked Victoria.

"We don't know. Never did, really. Your mother's sense of irony set in when she heard that Victoria thought it daft, so she began calling it hocus-pocus. So, that's what we both called it. Besides, calling it that has the added benefit of disguise. It's a bit like that story in Greek mythology where the name of the daughter of Demeter and Poseidon couldn't be revealed except to those initiated into her mysteries. So, she was called Desponia. Basically, Desponia means mistress of the house, which doesn't reveal a whole lot does it?"

"And," added Victoria, "Desponia wasn't her real name anyway! All right Daddy, hocus-pocus it is!"

SEVENTEEN

"Hello? Dormier? Wake up soldier!" Montgomery turned at the sound of Privet's voice. She saw Private Dormier pull herself out of the dream and open her swollen eyes.

"You crying, for God's sake, Dormier?" asked Privet.

"No, Captain Privet. No, ma'am."

"Well, good, because we're going to be moving camp tonight and I'll need your help."

"Help, ma'am?" Her body felt as though a few rounds from a Mauser rifle had hit her, but a slight movement confirmed to her that the worst of it was her right shoulder.

"Yeah, I want you to help pack up," said Privet. "I'm kidding Dormier."

"Oh, good. Thank you ma'am for just kidding."

"Dormier, I'm having you moved to a bigger field hospital near Port Elizabeth—"

"Oh! No, please! Please ma'am, let me stay. I'm almost completely recovered."

Monty continued to watch this exchange and smiled. Privet was a natural-born leader with a sense of humor—rare to have both qualities in the same person.

"Right, I see that. Seriously, Dormier, I'll do the joking around here. We're moving around midnight. I just need you to fill me in on a couple details."

"Details, ma'am?"

"Details, Dormier. Like next of kin. Where I can send a letter to let your family know you've been hit, but you're going to live. For now," she added, grinning.

"Ah, right. Well, just send my father a note then," said Victoria, "but don't say anything to frighten him, of course. Please ma'am."

"Naturally," said Privet. "Of course frightening him might prove slightly difficult since he's dead. You did know your father was dead, right, Dormier?"

"Dead," she repeated. "Right. Dead Daddy. Yes ma'am, I do know."

"And so then am I quite right in reminding you that he's actually been dead for several months now?"

"Yes. Yes, ma'am. March 21, 1900."

"So, Dormier, good, now that we've got that cleared up. Next of kin?" Privet took her small notebook out and wet the tip of her pencil with her tongue. She held the pencil at attention, ready to write. Her head was down. There was nothing but silence. She waited. Finally, she looked up.

"Next of kin, Dormier?"

Her brothers? Her sister? Oh Lord, no! She'd need someone with the power to actually keep her in Africa. "Ah, yes, well, I suppose that would be the Queen, ma'am."

"The Queen?"

"Yes, ma'am, Queen Victoria. My auntie."

Montgomery watched as Privet turned on her camp cot and called out to her.

"I thought you said she was no longer delirious, Monty?"

Montgomery stood up and walked slowly across the room from her makeshift desk to Victoria's bed. "The Royals bit?" she asked.

Privet nodded. Even Victoria nodded.

Montgomery shrugged and waved one arm as if to call forth some higher power. "She was talking the same way when she was delirious," she said. "Who's listed as her next of kin?"

Privet looked at her book. "Some fellow named A.V. Guelph."

"That's my auntie," Victoria said. "Her full name is Alexandrina Victoria. Guelph is her family name. All House of Saxe-Coburg and Gotha, of course."

"Oh, of course," said Privet. "Monty, would you step outside with me a moment?" As Privet stood to leave the infirmary, she asked another question. "Is this address correct for your auntie?" She held the notebook up to Victoria's face. "Is that right, WinCas?"

"Yes, ma'am. That's short for Windsor Castle."

"Auntie's house. Right?"

"'Fraid so, ma'am. Let me ask you, ma'am, if I were to be all recuperated, I mean completely well, mobile and irrepressibly coherent by midnight, would you be willing to forego the letter to next of kin? I'd so hate to worry the old girl."

Privet looked at Victoria closely, but she nodded. "Not

94

a problem, Dormier. Let's see how you're doing around midnight."

Privet turned to exit the tent and rolled her eyes at Montgomery and the nurse standing at a dressing station just inside the flap. Before following Privet outside, Monty turned toward her patient in time to see that Private Dormier rolled her eyes too.

EIGHTEEN

Victoria drifted in and out of a light sleep, images of her father waking her with a start. What a lovely man he had been! How could any man ever be quite as good? Even her two brothers, whom she adored, were savages compared to their father. Well, they were fully scalawags, anyway, although fiercely protective of Victoria and her sister. Beyond that, both Ambrose and Robbie had a wicked sense of humor and were fond of suggesting Victoria was just "one of the boys."

"And I mean that in the most favorable sense," Ambrose once remarked.

"I'm sure you do, Brosie, but I'd rather you not encourage Victoria in that vein," their father had said.

"No, of course, not, Father," agreed Ambrose, who made a face at the other occupants in the room as soon as his father turned away. Ambrose, the oldest of the four offspring was nearly 25, Rob was 23, Alexis was 21 and Victoria was 18.

Victoria opened her eyes as she felt the pulling pain of her wound, her shoulder muscles in a firestorm of attack under her skin. She'd have to do something about that. No one was in the infirmary, but Victoria could hear the muffled tones of lowered voices outside the front flap of the tent. She'd have to be quick, and she'd have to be successful, or they'd send her back to England for sure. Turning her head to the small utility table at her bedside, she saw her shoulder bag slung over one of the knobs to the single drawer that held common medical supplies.

Steadying herself, she slowly sat up in bed, reached for the bag and found the small leather pouch inside. She took the crystal from it and placed it on her damaged shoulder. She concentrated on the feel of the glass against her fingers and focused its increasingly cold surface directly on her shoulder. She sat that way for less than five minutes until the sounds of someone walking up the wooden steps to the infirmary's front flap caused her to put the crystal away quickly.

"Sitting up already, are we?" asked St. James.

"Yes, ma'am, good for the circulation, don't you think?"

"I do indeed, Private, though it might be a bit soon. I'll redo your dressings in a couple hours. Why not rest for now?"

Victoria nodded, glad to get the attention off herself. She rested her head on the pillow and watched as Clare St. James walked across the room to a small desk and sat down to shuffle some paperwork into neat stacks. As one of two full-fledged doctors, St. James took the opposite shift from Montgomery on the medical ward, such as it was.

St. James is a pretty woman, she thought, but she

always seemed just a little sad. Before Victoria could take that thought any further, her eyes closed and the world spun on without her knowledge for another two hours as the soldiers in Africa welcomed the sundowner winds, which was the closest thing the warriors of the Boer War could call a breeze.

St James' attention wandered from the endless stack of reports on her desk to the sleeping soldier, her only patient. The sun was down, but the warm breeze had diminished to a wisp, leaving the infirmary close and stuffy. St. James turned up the lights in the tent, opened the side vents and began to make a bit of noise. Victoria shifted in her bed but still slept. The wounded princess, St James thought. Well, she must be a princess if the Queen were her aunt. St. James decided to let Private Dormier wake naturally. She stepped outside the tent and saw Privet leaning up against an ambulance parked outside the infirmary. "I'll have one of those," St. James said, indicating the cigarette hanging from Privet's lips.

"Bad for the lungs," Privet said.

"Right. But good for the soul." St. James reached over and took a cigarette from the package Privet held out. St. James reached out, pulled Privet's cigarette from her lips, and lit her own from it. Pulling a deep drag, she replaced Privet's between her lips.

"Help yourself," Privet said with a smirk.

St. James looked at Privet with eyes narrowed by the smoke. "I usually do," she answered.

The two women stood there in silence, Privet relaxed against the lorry, St. James looking idly up into the twilight sky. She's easy to be around, thought St. James. "Any news from headquarters on Dormier?" she asked.

Privet stubbed out her cigarette with her boot. "Well,

yes. Turns out the little rascal is the Queen's niece, after all. And I've no idea how she ended up here, so save your breath on that one. But here's the clincher."

"Good Lord! That wasn't the clincher?" St. James shook her head and took another drag.

"Right? No, here's the payoff: Her Royalness just happened to shoot down a rare prototype—no, a one-of-a-kind!—German observation balloon, injuring a much-decorated German officer and personal friend of Kaiser Wilhelm who happened to be along for the ride." She slumped against the ambulance. "We couldn't be in any more trouble," she added.

"I suppose our Queen, the Kaiser's grandmother, has sent on her regrets?"

"Our Queen and most of the British High Command has sent its regrets to the Kaiser," said Privet. "Wilhelm loves his grandmother, but he's terribly resentful of the rest of his family, including his own mother."

"Lovely boy, that Kaiser," said St. James. "Speaking of the Royals, do we know how she did it? And who shot at her?"

"No idea how she did it," said Privet, "but her shoulder wound was probably from one of the snipers. Despite the Kaiser's support of the Boers, we're not actually at war with Germany—but shooting down their balloon could change that! Evidently the German High Command in Berlin has sent a strongly worded objection to Lord Salisbury." Privet shrugged. "A real mess."

"I can't imagine the esteemed Prime Minister Salisbury will be pleased. Any word about his son?"

"No," said Privet. "Lord Edward is in Mafeking gathering boys as messengers."

"I beg your pardon?"

"Lord Edward has figured out how to use the locals as messengers, and he's got himself a full brigade of nine-year-olds running through fire delivering orders from Colonel Baden-Powell to the infantry."

"I see," said St. James. "Well, with Baden-Powell, one never knows what's really happening. B-P's secret weapon is ruse and trickery. He loves it. I haven't heard much about Lord Edward other than he's second in command."

"Second in command of what, is the question," Privet said. "Best I can tell, B-P's just keeping him out of the way and out of the line of fire. I doubt B-P would want to have to write the 'we regret to inform you' letter to *those* parents."

St. James raised her hands in supplication. "What the hell, Privet! We've the Queen's niece in the infirmary, after she shot down the Queen's grandson's best friend. Then we've got Prime Minister Salisbury's son in the Boer cannon sights, and Kaiser Wilhelm, said grandson, milking his sorrow to more effectively play both sides. Is war meant to be practice for something? Something bigger?"

"I'd say it's practice for running the world," quipped Privet.

"Well, I'd say: Who wants to be part of that world?" St. James batted the air with her right hand. "These people," she finished.

"They haven't seen what you've seen, Clare. Not the way you've seen it. They haven't had to clean up the guts, mop up the blood and take off the arms and legs hanging by a crushed tendon."

"They see it on the battlefield! People like Lord Edward could report to mummy and daddy. He could tell them what it's really like out here."

"Oh, they know what it's like out here," said Privet. "But for the greater good of the Empire, they're trained not to complain."

"They're trained to lie, then," said Clare.

"That too," agreed Privet.

"All the sides agreed not to shell on Sundays, and look what's happening in Mafeking! How long before the Boers begin shelling our field hospital?"

"Tonight or tomorrow," said Privet, looking up at the cloud cover. "After what Dormier did, no telling what kind of retaliation we're in for."

"She's so young," St. James said. It was barely a whisper, but Privet heard the compassion in the medic's voice. "I'm sure she thought she was doing the right thing."

"Right. Unfortunately, I'm meant to move her out tonight, no matter what condition she's in. Lord Kitchener's involved now, and he wants to be able to tell the German Empire that blowing their balloon to bits was a tragic accident and the perpetrator has been removed from service."

"They're taking Dormier out of service?" asked St. James. "She's your best messenger."

"Well, when B-P found out we had the Queen's niece in our medical contingent, he ordered her removed for her own safety. I don't think the Germans know exactly who shot down their airship, and I don't imagine Kitchener is keen to have them find out. He approves of B-P's order. I wonder if Sir Edward agrees, though."

"Oh, Kitchener's a fine one to criticize!" said St. James. "If it were up to him, the entire Transvaal would be burned to the ground and all its citizens penned up like cattle in his holding camps. Refugees. Prisoners treated like criminals."

Privet glanced at St. James. She'd never seen her this fatalistic. War fatigue? Had to be hard on doctors who couldn't save every life. "Well, we follow the orders, St. James. Those other fellows make the rules." Privet gave her companion a modified and mock salute and started to walk up the stairs to the infirmary.

"Wait! Wait...Rosemary, please. Let me change her dressings first. I'll feel better about what you're going to say to her if I see she's improved."

"And if she hasn't?"

"Then I'll still feel like hell, so there's a chance I could feel better."

"In that case, I'll tell her after you change the dressing. I'd love to see you feeling better, Doctor, if only for a while."

Privet held the flap for St. James, who brushed past her with a small, mischievous smile and a rose-hued blush that made Privet blink.

NINETEEN

When Victoria awoke, two familiar faces were staring at her in what she would have considered disbelief. She knew then that the crystal had done its job—or rather, together with the crystal, she had done her job.

"I don't suppose you have any explanation for this, do you Dr. St. James?" asked Privet.

"None. None at all. Dormier?"

"Yes, ma'am?"

"Do you, Dormier?" asked St. James

"Do I what, ma'am?"

Privet leaned in closer. "Do you have any bloody explanation for the fact that there is no evidence of a shoulder wound, Dormier?"

Victoria craned her neck slightly to look at her shoulder. "A miracle, Ma'am?"

"Rather doubt it, Dormier," said St. James.

"Well, there's still a bit of blood," said Victoria,

pointing to a square area where the wound had been.

"Right, and that's just seepage from the dressing, because there *was* a wound under that dressing, Private." St. James held Victoria's gaze, neither of them blinking.

Finally, Privet spoke. "Awfully glad you've recuperated, Dormier. Saves me the trouble of writing to Auntie."

"Oh! I'm terribly glad about that," said Victoria. She smiled at both officers.

"Actually, I wouldn't have had to write, anyway."

Victoria held her breath. Her face remained placid, but her heart was fluttering. She said nothing, so Privet continued. "It seems your auntie has discovered your whereabouts—evidently she didn't know where you had got off to and South Africa was not on her list of possible destinations."

Victoria exhaled. The jig was up. Bloody hell and a half-bit banger, she swore silently. I still haven't made contact with Jack!

"Auntie knows, then?" Victoria finally asked. She decided to couch her equivocation in a question.

"Indeed." Privet offered one of her rare smiles. *She's smiling.*This couldn't be a good sign, thought Victoria.

"How did she find—I had left her a note. Well, a brief note, anyway."

"Really?" said St. James. "That was thoughtful of you." She looked at Privet. "Dear Auntie Queen Victoria, I believe I'll go on down to Africa and see what all the commotion is about."

Privet let out a guffaw. "Good one, Doctor!"

"Actually I said, 'Don't worry, Auntie, see you soon.'"

"And you wrote that note how long ago, Dormier?" St James stood as she asked.

Victoria's eyes studied the ceiling as if it were a calendar. "About six months ago?"

"Are you asking us, then?" said Privet. "You think it might have been six months ago?"

"Around that time," Victoria said.

"Rather knocks the hell out of 'see you soon,' doesn't it Dormier?" said St. James.

"Rather...mmm, yes. Yes ma'am."

Victoria learned that the flying fortress she had shot out of the sky belonged to her cousin Kaiser Wilhelm. Well, it belonged to his country, Germany, but it was almost the same, wasn't it? Worse, his dear friend Baron von Talbert and the pilot were severely injured when they jumped out of the basket. Four broken legs.

"And in fact, Dormier, Captain Clark's report indicates there were two airships in the vicinity, nearly identical," said Privet.

"No kid?" asked Victoria. "Uh, no kid, ma'am?"

"No kid, Private. So, naturally, we wondered, as you were in such a fighting spirit, why didn't you take them both down?"

"Oh, I did, Ma'am!" Victoria raised her right arm, pointed a finger at the sky and pretended to shoot twice.

"Funny thing is, Dormier, there's no sign of the second balloon having hit the ground," said Privet. "In fact, the Germans tell us they did not have another ship in the skies at that time.

Victoria nodded, and then shrugged. "Perhaps I just thought I shot two air ships," she offered. "Otherwise, ma'am, it's a complete and utter mystery!"

"Brilliant of you to reload after those two shots, though," mused Privet.

Victoria winced. "Maybe...maybe, hmm, it was all a

blur for me, ma'am. Another mystery, hmm."

"Oh, actually, Dormier, the only mystery we have now is how to get you safely to Port Elizabeth and eventually Cape Town for the excursion back to England. You'll be sent to Port Elizabeth, first, though. I'm thinking—"

"Back to England, Captain Privet? Why would I be going back to England?"

"Because you've nearly caused the collapse of the entire British Empire," Privet said. "But, more importantly, if I may presume to re-order the priorities, your auntie commands it. She demands to see you as soon as is humanly possible."

"Oh." Victoria looked at both officers and smiled. Surely Auntie had ordered Jack back to England, too. But she'd like to be certain of that. A moment later, she closed her eyes.

"Are you going back to sleep, Private?" asked St. James.

Opening her eyes, Victoria sighed. "No, Ma'am, just thinking of England."

TWENTY

Alice Ponsonby stepped into the officers' tent. It wasn't exactly a private club, but it was a momentary respite from the drudgery of front-line fighting.

"Ah, Pierce, there you are old chap!" shouted Swales. "Thought you'd be dead by now!"

Alice smiled and in her best Jack voice said, "Bloody hell to you, too, Jimmy Swales! Pour me one?"

Swales got a fresh glass from the makeshift sideboard situated behind the equally makeshift raw timber table.

Alice sat on the bench seat and hunched over her whiskey. She took a fast gulp then set it down hard for a refill.

"Got a bit shaken up on that last one, eh, Jack?" asked Swales. "I saw it blow, and I thought it would rain hell on you and your men."

Alice looked up, took a smaller sip of the whiskey and shook her head. "No, I knew it was off to our left and just a bit behind us. Looked like it was right overhead though, I'll give you that."

"Damn, man, it did indeed," said Swales. He poured himself another whiskey and gestured to Alice.

"No, I'm good. I'm off until morning, but we're moving our line back. My men are on it now."

"Back? Why the bloody hell back? Boers just took off running to beat the band when that bird blew! What do you know, Pierce?"

"Nothing. Just my orders, Jimmy. We lost Hardinage and Cunningham. But Colonel Morse said the Boers will double back on our flanks. Even when they run away, they're on you different the next time."

"So you saw the big balloon go up in flames?

Alice looked at Swales' bloodshot eyes and nodded.

"What do suppose happened? I heard it belonged to the Kaiser?"

Alice looked up sharply. There was something she didn't know. "Where'd you hear that, Jimmy?"

Swales paused and then shrugged. "Couple of seniors came in earlier and were talking. I guess it could cause a tremendous row between the Queen and her grandson."

"Ah, well then, maybe the Kaiser shouldn't be flying over Granny's battlefields with his big cigar!"

Swales looked shocked.

"Just between you and me, right Jimmy?"

"Right, Jack." Swales finished off his whiskey and stood up. "See you later, Jack!" Swales gave a mock salute and left the tent.

Alice mumbled. *Sure, Jimmy, see you later, snitch.* She knew he'd run to his mates and talk about Jack's verbal disrespect for Her Majesty. Alice sighed. The dirigible blowup had to be Victoria Dormier's handiwork.

Something with optical illusions, mirrors—Alice wasn't sure. But she knew of Victoria's Magick abilities. Indeed, Alice, thought, we are counting on them—but not to start a war with Germany for Christ's sakes! Victoria. Ah, how she missed her. But she had to get them both out of here, had to get them back to England. Each day she wondered how long she could keep up the disguise. Alice knew Her Majesty would send someone to find her, but she never thought the Queen would send Victoria! What a bolloxed up mess this is turning out to be. Had to be Victoria, though. Alice stood up, adjusted her uniform and exited the tent. As she was hailing a ride back to her men, she heard the shouts.

"They got one of the drivers!" someone yelled as he ran past Alice.

"Sir, Lieutenant Pierce, Sir!" another young man saluted. "A message for Officer in Command, sir. That's you, now, sir! Colonel's asleep, said not to be disturbed even if the whole continent blew up. Sir!"

Alice ripped open the envelope and saw a woman's handwriting. She scanned the brief note and saw that it was from Rosemary Privet, head of the Nurses brigade. Privet needed a couple men to help them move camp later that night. Alice made a noise and smiled. The messenger looked at her oddly, so she dismissed him.

She couldn't spare two men, but she could lend a hand herself. This should be interesting. Alice left one of two other officers in charge. By the time anyone realized she was missing, she'd be on her way to England. Theoretically.

TWENTY ONE

Alice rode into the Nurses Brigade encampment on her motorbike. Pulling up in front of the CO's quarters, she shut the engine, hopped off and stamped some of the dust off her boots. She looked up just as Privet came out of the tent.

"Captain Privet," she said, saluting.

"At rest Lieutenant. You're a brave one, Pierce!"

"I hope so, ma'am. Why d'you say that?"

"Hell of a fiery day on the playing field, eh?"

Privet took out her pack of cigarettes and offered one to Alice. They stood there wordlessly as Alice lit both their cigarettes.

"Almost lost my best driver today," Privet said through a cloud of smoke. "Funny thing, she was taking a message to you. Well, to you or whoever was still alive and in command."

Alice's hand began to shake, so she held the cigarette well below eye level.

"Ah, sorry. Who was that? The driver I mean?"

"No one you know, I'm sure," said Privet. "Young girl just over from home a few weeks ago. Name of Dormier."

Alice swallowed. "How badly hurt is she, Captain?"

"Oh, she'll survive. Funny thing is, her wound is almost healed. Pretty damn much a miracle, I think. Anyway, she's being shipped home."

"You don't say? Why? If her wound's healing, I mean."

"Got orders from B-P himself."

"Ah, well then, if Baden-Powell says so, then, yes. When is she to leave?"

"Well, she's at infirmary sleeping off some drugs the doctor gave her. But, tonight. After the move tonight. We'll find a way to get her on the train to Port Elizabeth."

"Fancy that!" Alice said. "I'm leaving for Port Elizabeth myself. I came up here to lend a hand with your move, and I'll be leaving right after that. Can I help you with Dormier?"

"Could you? That would be swell, Pierce. I'm really hesitant to put her on that train alone."

Alice frowned. "I think she'd be safe enough from our own men."

"I'm not worried about them, Pierce! I'm not even too worried about the Boers. I'm worried she'll escape and show up here again tomorrow morning!"

"Ah, I see, bit of a temperament, I suppose. Well, how about this? Don't tell her I'm to accompany her. I'll just make sure I get in the same railcar as she's in so I can keep an eye on her."

"Perfect," Privet said, rubbing out her cigarette with her boot. "You might want to take a peek at her in the

111

infirmary. So you know which one to watch."

"Will do," Alice said. "Think I'll go freshen up a bit first, then help with the loading up for the move."

Privet waved Pierce away and laughed. "Honestly, it's almost all done. The girls handled it just fine soon as I said I had sent for a couple men! I guess you saw the big birds blown up to smithereens then?"

"Hard to miss it! Anyone know what happened?"

Privet looked in the direction of the front. "I think my driver, Dormier, brought them, or it, down. And then mysteriously had the presence of mind to reload her pistol before she hopped on her bike to head back here. Just before she got shot. Some are saying one airship, others swear it was two."

Alice looked in the direction of the front, too. "These new recruits are amazing, aren't they Captain? Well, I'll be off now."

"Keep an eye out, Pierce. These Boers are everywhere."

Alice nodded then turned around to look for the officers' tent. Privet smiled. "Only female officers here, Lieutenant. But go ahead into my tent. Everyone's off doing things." Alice saw a look of curiosity cross Privet's face. She turned and ducked her head in the direction of the officers' tent before further inquiry became problematic. She glanced back at Privet and saw her shrug to herself as she walked away.

Alice hopped up the two-tier wooden steps and entered the tent. It smelled like females. A faint odor of gardenia soap and various dusting powders filled the air. She used one of the metal bowls to wash her face and slick back her hair. She scooted toward the rear of the tent and saw a flap loosely tied. Peeking out, she almost cried with relief. A single stall privy had been erected. For once she didn't need to time her particulars to the comings and goings of men. Afterwards, she returned to the tent, washed her hands and then threw the water out the back of the tent. She wanted to use the gardenia soap but decided that wouldn't do. Soon, she told herself, soon.

TWENTY TWO

Alice walked nonchalantly to the infirmary tent. The smell of disinfectant reached her nostrils at the same time an attractive woman opened the flap to descend the stairs. The slight scent of jasmine wafted past Alice as the woman, an officer and apparently a doctor, smiled and walked past her. As they were the same rank, no salute was necessary. Alice stood outside the tent, leaning against the stairs as if relaxing. She looked up into the sky and through the trees saw the smallest smattering of high clouds. When she saw the doctor turn into another tent, Alice hopped up the stairs and sneaked inside the tent. The lighting was muted. There were eight beds, seven of them empty. The bed on the right was occupied, but the resident had an arm thrown over the face, so Alice slipped into the tent further to get a closer look.

And there she was. Victoria Dormier, fast asleep. Alice

stepped back into the shadow created by the wall of the tent. Victoria's breathing was easy, rhythmic and steady. Alice saw her move an arm down to her side, but Victoria's eyes did not open, her breathing did not change. Without wishing to push her luck, Alice began to back out of the shadows and turned and headed for the door flap.

"Dr. Montgomery?"

Alice froze but then stepped out of the tent, hopped down the stairs and ran behind an opposite tent. She hid there for several minutes. Then she heard Privet and the doctor climbing the steps to the Infirmary.

Close call. Just stay out of sight until tonight.

She was thirsty for some cold water but dared not go into the mess tent. She went 'round behind, though, and slipped into the tent through the rear flap where, as she figured, the stores of food and water were kept. She filled her canteen, drank it down in gulps and refilled it. Once outside the rear of the mess tent again, she watched the ambulance lorries, bikes and horses being lined up for the move.

The horses were first, followed by the lorries. She'd place herself in the front line of the bike brigade, and when one of the lorries continued on to the train platform, she'd ride with the rear guard, usually two cycles. No one would even question it. If they ran into an ambush...no, it was only a mile to the train station. She hoped their earlier humiliation at the hands of the British coupled with the shock of seeing the dirigible blow up would drive the Boers further back across the river. They might eventually try to outflank the British troops, but there were better places to pull that off than the open scrub-lined trail leading to the train.

Alice took another swig of her water and wiped her

brow of perspiration. The temperature was high today. She'd have to conserve her energy. A hundred feet from the trail where the Nurses brigade was preparing for the midnight move, Alice saw a small hedge of flowering shrub. It wasn't much, but it would offer some shade and some cover. She bent over and stepped gingerly through the tall grasses. When she reached the hedge, she found it to be a bit larger than she realized. It formed a half circle around some other tall grasses. She set her rucksack down and followed it to the ground. She was exhausted beyond thinking. Using the bag as a pillow, Alice Ponsonby fell asleep dreaming of Jack Pierce's dilemma.

TWENTY THREE

When Alice awakened, she was all alone. She stayed perfectly still for several moments, listening for sounds. There were none. How could she have slept through all the noise of the entire encampment on the move? She sat up, but it took a minute before her eyes became accustomed to what little light there was from the moon. She reached into her rucksack and drew out her canteen. The water was lukewarm, but she needed to drink it. After gathering her thoughts, she stood up and walked a few steps to relieve herself. She'd never be able to follow the trail in the dark, and the quietness all around her made her shiver. This was not an ideal place for a woman to be alone—especially one dressed as a British soldier. She had a decision to make. She could wait until dawn and easily follow the trail left by the wagons, bikes and horses. But she was not keen on a night in the woods, and she was impatient. She would set off now and hope to catch up with Privet's group before Victoria was put onto the train to Port Elizabeth.

A movement to her left, followed by one to her right, settled the question. She could hear the murmurs. She hunched down tight against the base of the hedge. Five feet away from her, a single file of about ten Boer soldiers walked quietly through the forest. After they had passed she breathed again. Five minutes earlier they would have found her squatting in the grass with her britches down and her bottom exposed. She looked around. There could be more—there were bound to be.

She suspected they were part of a larger group intent on flanking the British troops. They hadn't been run off at all—they'd been emboldened to come 'round the sides. They probably didn't know they were following the Nurses brigade, but when they discovered it, they'd leverage that knowledge to their advantage. They'd no doubt place themselves between the rear of the entire British force and the medical and supply lines, especially when they realized how many more British soldiers had been added to the effort.

They would, in effect, outflank the British and create an ambush of inestimable damage with slaughter on all sides. Alice knew that the guerilla tactics of the Boers were more effective by half against the regimented and awkwardly unwieldy British troops. She had to get a message to her men. But that meant returning in the direction of what had been the front. No telling what she'd run into, but it had to be done.

As she moved in stealth through what had been the Nurses' camp, she looked around for her bike. *Nothing. Wait!* She saw a hulk of something near the still-standing latrine. She watched it from within the tall grasses. She looked up. The moon was going to reveal her position any minute. She crouched down again, and then she saw it.

The door to the latrine opened, and a tall man stepped out. He lit a cigarette, cupping the flame, but in that brief flash, she saw her bike leaning against the side of the outhouse. If she could get to it without being seen, she'd have to roll it down the main road. Then she'd have to gun it up the hill, down the second hill and onto the flat lands in pursuit of her regiment. She was a good driver, but not as good as Victoria and she'd been shot!

The tall man walked in the direction of the others. She watched until he was out of sight, then breathed deeply. She should assume the Boers were all over this immediate area. She needed to create a diversion in case they were. She could still smell the tobacco.

She looked around. There wasn't much timber on the veldt, but there was plenty in this small area. She put her finger in her mouth and then held it up to the air. As she suspected, the slight breeze was blowing away from the road she needed to be on. All she had to do was get the bike, roll it to the road and set the woods on fire enough to damp the sound of starting her engine. Meanwhile, she contemplated crawling over to the bike on her belly. The idea did not appeal. But once she ran across the path toward the latrine, she was going to be in full view of anyone who had a rifle and a good aim. She wasn't Catholic, but she made the universal Church of Rome sign of the cross and took off running.

TWENTY FOUR

After Victoria was safely off to Port Elizabeth, the 32-member Nurses Brigade plus four officers spent the night packing up and moving their field wards to a location three miles behind their front line. From that position, they could set up individual first aid tents close to the left and right flanks. Then they'd set up a transport caravan to the rail lines that led to Port Elizabeth for the more seriously wounded.

Privet sent St. James to set up a forward infirmary tent a half-mile behind the front. It was primarily an evaluation and triage site staffed by a senior nurse and three junior ones.

"Hell, Captain, you're pushing pretty hard to get me killed! I'd have paid for my own dinner, you know."

"Not on my watch, you wouldn't have," said Privet. She looked around. She could smell the smoke from the gunpowder, hear the noise from the cannons. She wasn't happy sending St. James so close to the firepower, but she was the best doctor to assess the wounded. Besides, if a soldier needed immediate emergency surgery, St James was fast, talented and fearless in her determination to save a life.

"Easy for you to say," mumbled St. James, as she and a couple of the nurses hoisted the tent onto the platform. "Hey, Captain, this flooring is a half inch off the bloody dirt!"

"Best I could give you on such short notice," said Privet. "Trust me, you won't be staying long here, either."

"Sounds like I'm a goner, then," St. James said.

"Just keep your head down and your congeniality up, St. James!"

St. James waved away Privet's tease.

"Going to check the flanks. See you later, Doctor saint!"

Privet hopped on the back of a motorcycle driven by one of the messengers.

"How's Dormier, ma'am?" She revved the engine and brought her boots down hard on pedals.

"She'll live," shouted Privet. "West flank field tent first, Private."

The driver nodded and ten minutes later they pulled up alongside another field tent. A half hour later, they repeated the drill on the east flank.

A lorry, drivers and two messengers on motorbikes made up the staff at each of the flank locations. Horses were available, too, but the infantry coveted the warrior animals as transportation for their forward scouts.

From the main field ward, the closest rail line was three-quarters of a mile. With the guerrilla tactics of the Boers, no mode of transporting the injured was fully safe, but patients had a better chance of reaching Port Elizabeth by rail than by a horse-driven lorry.

Privet returned to the main field ward and saw Montgomery outside the tent with a small group of nurses. She waited for her to finish up with the field protocols. Montgomery dismissed the nurses with her usual cry.

"Save a life, ladies, one life at a time!"

"Yes ma'am, save a life, one life at a time!" they shouted in unison.

Montgomery ambled over to where Privet sat on a motorcycle.

"Juliet, when was the last time you had the leisure of trying to save one life at a time?"

"Well, Captain—"

"Oh, it's Captain now, is it?"

"Rosie," Montgomery corrected. "Rosie, I haven't had the leisure of trying to save one life at a time at any time since I arrived in this insect-infested, water-deficient, sand-shifting, blazing hot and freezing cold country. But I say that to them so they don't get overwhelmed when the blood starts running and the guts start spilling."

"How many you got in there," Privet said, indicating the ward.

"Just three right now. Nobody in terribly serious shape yet. Flesh wounds, one broken nose."

"A broken nose? Somebody get into a fight?"

"No, a young guy, first week here, tripped on his own tent peg."

"Jesus!"

"Uh huh. My sentiments exactly. How's Clare doing up front?"

"She's good. Not awfully happy so close to the

firepower."

"Well, she's the right one for that position. She can assess injuries and do surgery while drinking coffee and filling out reports."

Privet studied Juliet Montgomery in the ambient light from a nearby lantern. "You're a splendid doctor, Julie."

"Ah, thanks, but St. Bitch is better. Better under pressure, definitely, and if someone needs to be operated on to live long enough to be brought here, she's the best."

"I don't believe I've ever heard you call her that!" said Privet.

"I never have done," she said, "but I just wanted to see you smile."

What does that mean? Rosemary, not everything means something.

"Am I so deadly serious, then?" Privet asked after privately admonishing herself.

"You've been pretty serious the last 24 hours."

"I have, haven't I? Sorry. I wanted to get this move sorted out, get everyone in their places."

"You know something?" asked Montgomery.

"I might," said Privet.

"Will you be telling me anytime soon, Rosie?"

"I'll just tell you to get a good night's sleep," Private said. "And turn in early," she added.

Montgomery nodded. Privet wanted to say more, to tell her about the siege the next morning. Their troops were a half-mile away tonight, but by morning, they'd have passed the field hospital and be advancing in the pre-dawn hours for a surprise attack on the Boer stronghold, two miles away. Only this time the British had additional cannons and a thousand reinforcements.

How were a thousand men going to get past St. James'

field hospital to the front line without being seen? But maybe they weren't coming up from the rear. Maybe they would extend the flanks to encircle and ensnare the enemy this time. Privet didn't know the details, but she'd know by dawn when her orders came through. She expected to be counting dead bodies an hour after that.

TWENTY FIVE

When St. James heard it, she knew immediately what it was. It was dulled by thick grasses and a light wind, but there was no other sound like the steady stomp of boots cadencing on the ground in the dirgeful rhythm of a requiem yet unsung. At first she thought the sounds were off to her left, then she realized the thudding beat came from both sides of the flanks. She sat up in her cot. Something was happening. Or going to happen. She had gone to sleep feeling that way. Oddly, the sound of troop movements did not allay her presentiment.

She looked at her watch. 3:00 a.m. She'd fallen asleep immediately after the gnawing at her brain confounded her into exhaustion. Five hours sleep. No one was stirring, but she knew the sentries were hearing what she heard.

This might be a good time to write a letter, she

thought. But first, she would talk to the guards.

"It's our own, ma'am," one of the sergeants offered as he saw her step out of her tent.

"Figured it must be," she said. "Everyone rested, everyone ready?"

"Yes, ma'am. Don't know how much sleep the last bunch will get, just sent them to their tents an hour ago, but this group's as rested and ready as they're going to be."

"Right. Good, Sergeant. Ready for what, I'm not sure."

"Ready for war, ma'am."

"Right. Well, I'm going to get some coffee," she said, holding up her cup, "and write a letter. Have we got a post in the morning?"

"We normally do, ma'am."

"Normally?"

"Courier delivers at dawn and departs a quarter hour later, sooner if possible, later if we're taking fire."

"Oh, right. Right, Sergeant. Well, then, the coffee."

He saluted her smartly, and she returned the gesture.

St. James walked through the open flap of the canteen. The lanterns were set low, but the coffee was brewed. She saw a couple of soldiers hunched over a table, reading. They hadn't heard her.

"At ease, soldiers."

They jolted upright in place as she turned away from them to underscore her order. She warmed her hands on the heat of an oversized china cup that she carried everywhere. She took a sip of the black brew, peered through the dully lit tent at the young men and walked back to her tent.

How many will be alive by full daylight? Would she be alive?

What should she say? He wouldn't relate to anything she had to report. "I love you" seemed distant and far away when one was far away. He'd been against it, of course. Her coming down to Africa.

"Heathens and barbarians," he'd said. "Wouldn't mind having a few pieces of their gold or a few of their diamonds, though. Only reason to be there, far as I can see. Doesn't mean you need to be there, Clare, darling. Plenty of sick people right here in London."

But she knew what he really meant. He really meant she should stay in London, marry him, have his children and give up medicine. Oh, he wouldn't suggest it all right away, but they both knew he'd want that eventually. And why couldn't she just do it? Why not marry him, raise a family, maybe even have a small private practice. Nothing too demanding—nothing too time-consuming. Nothing she could love.

That was his main objection, wasn't it? She loved the Nurses Brigade too much. If she went to another theater of war, he'd say the same thing. And she certainly couldn't go traipsing off to war with babies at home. So what could she write? What could she say that wouldn't lead him to respond with a request that she give up her commission and return home?

And...maybe there was something wrong with her. Maybe she didn't love him enough. But she did! She knew she did. He was perfect in so many ways. He'd make a good father, he was a good provider...he was a sensitive and thoughtful lover. Oh, that's what she missed! She missed his strong arms around her, his soothing reassurances, his joyous outlook on life. True, he was a bit impatient with her when it came to her career, but hadn't he always seemed proud of her nonetheless?

127

"My fiancée, Dr. Clare St. James," he'd say by way of introduction to all.

St. James sipped the coffee and let the fragrant heat of its steam fill her senses. He had an important position in London as Solicitor Partner in an old established firm, and she was proud of him.

She held the pen above the paper. She had to sort it out with him. She had to let him know something about her love for him. She had to assure him that what she did was only part of who she was, but it was as important to her as the air she breathed. She had to assure him her heart was big enough to love him, to love their unborn babies and to pursue her love of medicine. And she'd give him the gift of not having to ask her to give up anything—after this campaign, she would resign her officer's commission. She would return to London, marry him, have his children and be a physician in London or whatever town in England he preferred. It was hitting her more every day: She hated war. She loved the Nursing Service, but she hated war. She began to write, filling up page after page of her feelings. Only the sound of cannons booming in the distant haze of a smoke-filled sunrise ended the letter.

Hastily, she put on a clean uniform. She dropped the letter in the camp post on her way to the hospital tent. She felt happy, relieved, in love. She hadn't been forced to make a difficult choice between husband and career, after all! She just had to let him know that medicine was her life blood and her love for him the oxygen to keep it flowing. But war? War was an infection that flowed through the blood stream until its poisons reached, then stopped the human heart.

TWENTY SIX

Victoria Dormier disembarked from the dirty, smelly and humid rail car and stood on a wooden platform in Port Elizabeth. She could smell the sea but couldn't see it. As she looked around, she saw British military troops, nurses, medics and other military support personnel milling around. The usual assortment of rail station vendors offered water, food and information.

Victoria adjusted her uniform tie and cap and walked toward a newspaper vendor. She listened for a moment as he spoke to a customer, and she wondered whether she was going to have a difficult time understanding the residents. They seemed to speak English, but their accent was so thick the mother tongue was nearly unrecognizable. She was to report to Field Hospital 8, but she had no idea where it was or how to get there.

A British officer approached her. "Need some help,

Private?" Victoria saluted smartly. "At ease, soldier."

"Thank you, Colonel. Yes, actually, I'm to report to the commanding officer at Field Hospital Eight, but I've no idea how to get there, sir."

"Well, Private"—he glanced at her nameplate— "Dormier, you are in luck. I'm the C.O. at Eight. Would you care to hitch a ride with me? Happy to give you a lift."

"How do you do, sir?"

"Colonel Parker, Dormier, pleased to make your acquaintance. Come along then, I have a driver here somewhere."

A black man in a long white cotton dress with billowy white trousers approached the colonel. He hefted the officer's large suitcase onto the back of a Benz Velo. The single bench seat was barely wide enough for the three of them. Dormier sat in the middle, between the driver and her C.O.

"What's your assignment then, Dormier?" he asked.

"Well, sir, I'm not sure. I was with the 2nd Battalion Worcestershire Regiment, and I was shot at delivering a message to Captain Hardinage."

"Ah, nasty business, that," Parker said. "Charles Cunningham was a good friend of mine."

"I'm sorry for your loss, air," Victoria said. "Lieutenant Colonel Cunningham and Captain Hardinage were killed within a half hour of one another trying to regain some of the earlier losses at Slingerfontaine. We lost a lot of good men there."

"What's this I heard about an airship being shot down? Don't suppose you know anything about that, though. It's meant to be all hush-hush, but you know how that goes."

Victoria saw that he was warming to his story, and she

was surprised, but complimented, that he'd decided to let her in on a state secret.

"Apparently was a messenger cyclist, shot the devil out of that thing so fast it crashed in flames inside a minute. Say, weren't you a messenger?"

"Oh yes, sir!" Dormier said, more enthusiastically than she felt.

"Well, evidently the whole brouhaha had something to do with the Kaiser—well, what doesn't, eh?"

Victoria frantically sorted through the dwindling options in her mind and decided diversion was her best defense. Her mother's words rang in her ears as though she were hearing them in the present. *No matter the circumstances, Victoria, never, ever reveal your power to any but one you love as dearly as your father and I love one another. Only to that person, darling, only that.*

"Sir, how long have you been here, if I may ask?"

"Here? Here in Africa or here in Port Elizabeth? Been in Africa two years, Port Elizabeth about two months. Miss the front, though. Well, I do and I don't. Plenty of carnage, but plenty of courage too. Our boys are putting in one helluva fight. Oh, excuse me, Private. Need to watch my language in front of the fairer sex, or so I've been told." Parker laughed at himself and turned his head toward his driver. "Bogarde, could you stop at the enlisted barracks for our soldier, here?"

"Yes, sir, happy to, sir."

"You'll like it here, Dormier. Plenty to do, plenty to see, and plenty to drink. If you imbibe, of course."

"On occasion, Sir. Rare occasion, but it's good to know, sir."

"Ah, here we are. These are the general barracks, and the drivers and messengers usually take up in the south

131

wing over there," he said, pointing to a section of the large tent building.

It stuck out at a right angle from the rest of the tent city, each section emblazoned with a bright red cross. It was built on a wooden platform like most of the medical facilities. The flagpole had several different colors flying a foot or so under the flag of the British Empire, which was bigger and brighter than the others.

"I'll check in on you, Dormier, make sure no one's giving you misinformation on how it is around here. And feel free to call on me, anytime. Anytime, dear girl, anytime."

Parker hopped out of the Velo and helped Victoria to step down. In an odd reversion to protocol over propriety, she turned to salute Parker. "Thank you, sir, thank you very much."

Parker returned a half salute and smiled. Victoria watched as they drove off.

"Bogarde, if you ever see that young private walking these dusty roads, be sure to give her a lift. My order, if anyone asks."

"Yes, sir, Colonel, I certainly will. Do you know her, sir?"

Parker stretched his legs and looked across the African veldt at the smeary sky above a dusty horizon. "Not really," he said, "but I'm on rather good terms with her auntie back home."

TWENTY SEVEN

After a few days in Port Elizabeth, Victoria found herself with so much free time she began to get anxious. *Where was Jack?* She thought she'd have seen him by now. She began to have Bogarde take her into the crush of the port where the sights and sounds and smells of British military men, horses, artillery and provisions were offloaded from the Queen's Navy ships on a round-theclock basis.

Victoria found a small outdoor plaza up a few steps from the main street. From here, she could watch the work on the wharves, drink the rich coffee and order a small plate of Vetkoek. Deep fried in oil, the pastries were often filled with mince or various jams and marmalades.

She loved to sit for hours at a time, watching and noting everything she could see. At first Bogarde would wait alongside the Velo, but after a day or so, it became obvious that Private Dormier was in no hurry to return to the base. He eventually agreed to leave her to her wanderings, returning several hours later to pick her up. That's when Victoria would leave the small plaza and roam through the inner pathways and lanes that fed into the central wharf area. She was looking for Jack, but it seemed he wasn't looking for her.

It was on one of these sojourns that she came upon the backside of a refugee encampment. Victoria stopped, frozen in place. Her eyes got wide as she watched the scene through a hole in a copse of privet hedge. A British soldier stood above a cowering woman who clasped two young children close. Two more, young boys, sat alongside their mother. All the children looked wilted, and one baby, in particular, seemed to be having trouble breathing. The soldier raised his voice, his demeanor threatening, and his tone angry. "You cannot, madam, be admitted to the hospital tent. You cannot take these children in there, and you ought not leave them here in the hot sun."

"And yet," she answered, "you leave us all here in the hot sun to die of thirst or drink the filthy water, to die of starvation or eat the stale crumbs." Her voice was clear, but she sounded fevered. "My daughter is in hospital, she is dying, and we wish to see her for one moment only before...before she is taken from us. I cannot leave these children alone, and they wish to see their sister. Please, officer?"

"I'm sorry, madam. I cannot make an exception. Please return to your tent."

The woman turned from him without a word and took her children inside a nearby tent. The soldier stood still in the hot, humid air, flies buzzing around him, his face reddening.

134

Victoria stuck her head through an opening in the green wall of leaves that hid her body. "Excuse me, Private," she said, "Why can't we allow her a moment with her dying child?"

He looked around to see where the voice was coming from. Then he spotted her, and she knew he could see a bit of her uniform, but he wouldn't have been able to determine her rank. She watched his face reflect the options his mind was reviewing. He stepped a few steps in her direction, and though his stance indicated his wariness, his tone revealed his decision to play it safe.

"Because ma'am, these women's husbands are out there in the veldt killing our countrymen. Countrymen and women," he added.

"In a civilized society, Private, warring forces are to allow the proper burial of their dead."

"Well, her daughter's not dead yet, is she ma'am?"

Victoria blanched at his callous disregard for another human being's grief. Then she heard a scratch in his voice as he continued.

"It's bad here, ma'am, but 'tweren't the English soldiers that made the Boer families' lives a living hell. These ladies' husbands are out there exploding the trains that's meant to bring our side food, medicine, blankets and tents. And some say the camp is far better than the filthy way they lived their lives before."

"I doubt they would agree, Private." Victoria began to back slowly out of the hedge.

"Where you from, ma'am, which group?"

Caught off guard, Victoria answered him truthfully, if not fully. "I'm up at Field Hospital Number Eight," she said. "Well, good-day, soldier."

She saw his eyes narrow in suspicion.

"Good-day ma'am." He gave a smart salute before walking in the other direction. Maybe he'd think her a nurse assigned to the hospital. He wouldn't be likely to ask around about a messenger.

Victoria walked slowly along the perimeter of the refugee camp. Every few meters the same or similar scenes played out between the British and their captives. She knew if she watched much longer she would be forced to intercede on the internees' behalf. But where would one begin?

She walked across the road and sat under the tree that faced the back of a small service building in the camp. The hot wind dried the sweat from her face. She could not believe what she had just seen. How was this war? Surely this isn't what the people back home thought was happening. They thought, they all thought, it was soldiers on soldiers, weapons on weapons, and yes, death on death, certainly, but among soldiers. Not innocent women. Not children, some just born, all facing sickness and probably death in the sordid camp conditions.

Why were there no proper lodgings? The threadbare tents were ripped and torn and scant protection from the sun, the wind and the rain. Why were there no gardens? These women were farmer's wives, they knew how to grow food, how to feed their families, how to coax the unforgiving soil into giving.

She wiped more sweat from her brow and tried to clear her throat from its dryness by coughing, but without water, her whole system felt wracked with dryness.

Water!

She jumped up and ran over to a different section of the fence surrounding the encampment. She could see people milling around in the center. Her eyes scanned the

THE GIRL WITH 2 HEARTS

periphery of the closest yard. She peered through the bushes, looking, searching, and willing herself to find it. And finally she did. Forty or fifty women and their children were crowded around a large metal tank, each of them dipping containers of various types and sizes into the tank. Two guards stood nearby watching the women, leaning in closer every few minutes as if to ensure that no one woman dipped her container more than once.

Water! Fresh, drinkable water! And little of it.

As she completed walking the perimeter of the camp, she saw a placard above the entrance that identified this hellish site as Port Elizabeth Refugee Concentrated Camp. Well, now she had a name to go along with a location that most resembled Hell. Victoria whipped around and ran as fast as she could to the town center where she knew her driver would be waiting. Somebody was going to hear about this. Somebody important.

As she retraced her steps to the plaza, she saw Bogarde pacing nervously in front of it.

"The C.O. wants to see you immediately," he began. "And it does not look good for Private Dormier, I must say. I don't know the details."

Victoria hopped up into the Velo of her own strength. "Good," she snapped, "because I want to see the C.O., too."

Bogarde raised his eyebrows.

"I just saw the Concentrated Camp where all the Boer women and children are. I cannot believe that we, the English, are treating human beings in that manner. Women and children! And old men!"

Bogarde nodded but made no response. Victoria saw that he glanced over at her a couple times during the drive to Base. She liked Bogarde. She might be able to have

Colonel Parker look into things. Otherwise, she'd go right up the chain of command. Victoria mentally composed her letter. *Dear Auntie...*

TWENTY EIGHT

Dormier walked into the barracks in time to see that a mandatory general assembly had been called for a quarter hour hence. She splashed some cold water on her face, straightened her uniform and made it to the assembly with a minute to spare.

Colonel Parker paced in front of the assembled group of nurses, ambulance drivers, medics and the few doctors he had been able to cull from the ships in the harbor. The clock on the wall said 7 p.m.

Parker's head was down as he walked back and forth at the front of the room, absently biting his lower lip. Suddenly he stopped at mid-point and looked out at the forty or so people gathered before him. All of them became immediately silent. Their somber faces foretold the nature of the announcement Parker was about to make.

"The first two cars are on their way. Arrival estimated at 2200," he said, "if they don't get attacked. Intelligence reports 67 seriously wounded—a great deal of limb damage, brain concussion and blindness. Another 140 are moderately wounded but mostly mobile. That's 207 soldiers arriving in less than three hours. And about forty of us. You know the drill, especially with transporting the worst first, not an easy task as they've been bundled and trundled willy-nilly into these rail cars. Are you ready ladies and gentlemen?"

A chorus of "Yes, sir!" filled the tented room. En masse, they saluted him.

"Dismissed to your stations!" he answered, saluting in rejoinder.

As everyone was filing out of the tent, Victoria stood off to the side watching Colonel Parker speak to one of his captains. She intended to discuss the internment camps with him. Seeing her, Parker motioned for her to approach.

"Sir," she said, with a salute.

"At ease, Private. You can ride, can't you?"

"Sir?"

"A motorcycle, Dormier, you can ride one of those contraptions, right?"

"Oh, yes sir!"

"And rather well from what I've heard!"

Dormier's lips pursed as she held in her answer. *Better than any man here.*

"Here's what I want. I want you to ride to the port, find the Harbor Master and tell him to let seven more ships disembark tonight. Captain Knowles will give you my written orders."

"Yes, Sir! Right away sir!"

"And Dormier?"

"Sir?"

"Simply to the port and back. No side adventures."

"Yes, sir."

"Good, now get that pretty face headed toward the water! Um...oh sorry, Dormier, you understand, of course, old habits and all that!"

"Perfectly, sir! I understand perfectly! Thank you for the assignment, sir. Goodbye sir!"

"Safe trip, Dormier," Parker said gruffly. Turning to Captain Knowles, Parker barked out an order.

"Pen my orders, Captain, and have one of your men find her the best machine you've got." Knowles saluted, and as he turned to leave, Parker motioned for Victoria to follow him.

She stood off to the side as he wrote the Colonel's orders. He signed the chit and handed it to one of his men, who ran back in the direction from which they had just come.

"As soon as the orders are signed, your transportation will be ready miss. I'm giving you my personal motorcycle."

Victoria stood straight and stiff but did not respond.

"At ease, Private. I hope you can handle her—she's big."

"Thank you, sir. I can handle her, sir."

The man with the orders returned, and after Knowles had placed the paper in a sealed envelope, he handed it to Victoria. "Guard it with your life, Private. We don't want the Boers to know our plans."

Victoria saluted and turned to go outside. Knowles followed her but stayed on the steps to the large tent. When she saw the motorcycle, she smiled. It was big, yes, but not the biggest she'd ever driven. She could tell, though, it was faster than what she was used to. She slung her leg over the saddle, grabbed the handles and jumped it, pleased to hear it roar immediately to life. Even in this sub-Saharan hell, this machine had been well taken care of. Captain Knowles nodded, and without hesitation, Victoria tore into the black night like a woman possessed.

"I guess she can sure ride," the junior officer said to Knowles.

"Sure looks that way," he answered. "Good. I want my cycle back."

TWENTY NINE

The hot wind seared her face, but the sand, kicked up by the motorbike, stung. Victoria peered into the darkness as far as her single headlight would allow. Anything could cross her path, jump out at her, fire at her, kill her. She leaned in tighter over the handlebars, her knees gripping the gas tank, her heart beating fast. She should still have had a word with Colonel Parker about that camp. Who could have known her first opportunity would turn into a special mission that other lives depended on?

She saw the dull glow of vapor lamps and fires in the sky ahead. Must be three more miles to the port. As the lights disappeared behind an upcoming ridge, Victoria glanced up at the sky. She sat up a little in the seat. Her way was lit by a nearly full moon and billions of stars. The narrow road was empty, but she still felt vulnerable. She reached up to her goggles and readjusted them. Feeling her posture creating drag on the motorcycle, she leaned in low and tight again.

She went from the empty desert to the busy, crowded and noisy wharf. She pulled up in front of the wharf master's dwelling, a sparse one-room building made of rough timber. She saw several longshoremen hanging around the front of the building.

"Which way to the military adjutant's station?" she asked.

They looked at her, startled, then suspicious. She realized what the problem was, and removed her goggles and helmet.

"On assignment from Col. Alfred Parker," she added.

Wordlessly they pointed to another, larger building a couple dozen yards away. She saw a couple military guards at the door and walked her motorbike toward the office. Two Military Police came to attention.

"Your business, please, ma'am?" one of them said.

"Delivering a message from Colonel Parker," she said. She waited outside while one of the MPs went inside. He was back in seconds and held the door for her.

Inside, an officer was escorting an attractive woman to the door through which Victoria had just entered. After the lady had departed, the officer glanced at Victoria

She saluted. "Sir, a communication from Colonel Parker, sir!"

"At ease," he said, waving a hand in minor dismissal.

He took the letter from her, read it quickly and raised his free hand to his forehead. "How the bloody hell am I meant to empty seven ships of men, horses and supplies?" he asked no one in particular. "Sanders!" he called out. As he re-read the missive, another officer came out of a rear office door.

"Sir?"

"Parker says send him seven ships' worth. Now! Today! Tonight!"

The officer looked at him in shock. "Tonight, sir? Yes, sir! That will take about five days working 'round the clock. Most of the longshoremen are on half shifts, sir."

"Aren't we paying them, Lieutenant?"

"Yes, sir, but they are not partial to the English, sir."

"Pay 'em double, then," snarled the Captain. "See if that dislodges their Boer sympathies. To it, Lieutenant! And Sanders? Keep those damn suffragists and pacifists out of my office! I just had another one in here."

With a salute, the junior officer left the room. The Captain was scrawling something on his stationery. He placed a single page in an envelope and handed it to Victoria.

"See Colonel Parker gets this immediately," he commanded.

"Yes, sir.

"Well, don't dawdle, Private...Dormier. To it then!"

Victoria saluted and pivoted for a quick departure. She ran back to where she had parked her motorbike. *Why can't Auntie put more women in charge of things? Must speak to her about that.*

***

She was thinking. Driving her motorcycle through the oil-black desert, thinking about the lady in the Duty Office. The Duty Officer had called her a pacifist. And a suffragist. Well, pacifists were for peace and suffragists were for women's rights, so what could be wrong with that, Victoria wondered. She thought about the mother in the camp. Damn!

She wasn't going fast. The message had been delivered and the urgency was gone. Still, she'd like to return this motorcycle to its owner. It was cooler, almost chilly, and the stars formed a giant chandelier of crystals, blinking and shining and shooting just for her. She wasn't sure what other duties Colonel Parker had in mind for her, but she knew, as she crested the hill that—Oh God!

Victoria tried to brake, but it was too late. She hit the blockade of wagons stretched across the road and was thrown into the air. She didn't remember hitting the ground, but when she regained consciousness, her sense of smell was assaulted by burning wood. She heard a commotion as hairy arms and darkened faces pulled her from the wreckage. And then she passed out again.

When she awoke, the blazing sun was burning the fair skin on her arms, both of which felt broken. She moved her fingers, relieved to see they did move. Peering through eyelids swollen half shut, she saw the source of her problem. Six or seven men stood around holding the bridles of the horses that apparently had been connected to the wagons at some point. They muttered in a guttural tongue that she recognized as more Dutch sounding than anything. *Afrikaans.* Occasionally one of the men would raise his voice and several others looked over at her. She remained motionless and, to the untrained eye, unconscious.

She would love a drink of water. As her legs began to fall asleep, she gingerly flexed muscles in both legs. She wiggled her toes in her boots. She inched the fingers on her right hand toward the pocket in her pants to check on her leather case, when two strong arms seized her wrists from behind and hoisted her up upright.

"Wat het ons hier? 'N meisie verken?"

What have we here? A girl spy?

The other men laughed.

"Leave her alone, she's worthless," another said in English.

"Hmm. Miskien. Miskien nie," the burly one said as he let go of her arms.

Maybe. Maybe not.

Victoria slumped back onto the ground and scooted backwards to a nearby boulder. It was half in the shade, and she let them see by her body language that she was trying to find shade. *Boers.* Boers had captured her.

One of them handed her a canteen. She took two large gulps and handed it back to him. He seemed surprised, even impressed.

"Show me your identification," he said.

She reached around into her back pocket and pulled out a thin leather envelope. She handed it to him. He pulled out two documents and read them.

"In Her Majesty's service," he read to the others. "That makes her the enemy."

"Dit maak haar ons gevangene," the other said. He smirked.

That makes her our prisoner.

"Well, Private, I think he's right. You are our prisoner."

She nodded.

"You do speak English, Private?"

She was reluctant to speak but could not see another alternative. "I do," she answered. "But I'm just the messenger."

"En wat was die boodskap?" the big one said.

"He wants to know what message you delivered."

"I don't know. I'm not allowed to read them. I just deliver them."

"To?"

She licked her lips.

"Sy lieg!" shouted the big one.

"He says you're lying, Private. What do you say to that?"

Realizing her error, she pointed to the canteen. And licked her lips again, but this time it wasn't from nerves, it was thirst from a burning desire to throw them off. The English speaking one turned to his comrade.

"Ek dink nie so nie. Sy is dors."

I don't think so. She's thirsty.

The big one made a guttural snarling sound but turned away. Victoria took one large swallow of water and handed the canteen back to the Boer. As she brought her arms down, she rested them against her sides, hoping to feel her leather case in her pocket. It was slender, and all the apparatus inside folded flat to keep it that way. She felt it. Now, what to do about this?

After removing the wagons from the road and hiding them in a gully off to the side of it, all the men sat under whatever bush shade they could find. The trained their spyglasses in the direction of Port Elizabeth. They seemed to be waiting for something. No vehicles of any kind travelled the road, and Victoria thought that alone was odd. By now, she reasoned, the trains with patients should have arrived at Base Hospital 8. And in another few hours, or sooner, long transports of men, machinery, weaponry and animals should be coming along from disembarkation at Port Elizabeth.

She looked around. Nothing but flat desert and a few small bushes. Then, more for inspiration than anything, she looked up at the sky. The first one she saw was small. But it was gathering density. She smiled at the grey-white opacity. She needed that cloudbank to grow, and she needed to devise a means to get at least ten feet away from this band of Boers.

Judging from the sun, it was late afternoon. She figured she had about 45 minutes of good daylight left. It all depended on how fast the cloudbank grew. It was coming from Port Elizabeth to the east but a bit north of the narrow highway. Then, too, the British troops could be less than a mile away headed toward Field Hospital 8 and the front. Victoria realized she didn't have enough information to make an educated guess. If they weren't on the highway, her plan wouldn't work. If they were anywhere close, it also wouldn't work. She needed those cloud banks to move up and past her position.

When she could not chance any further delay, she spoke to the English speaking Boer. He walked toward her, accompanied by a young man who looked a lot like him. She explained her need to relieve herself and expressed the hope they would allow her some privacy...perhaps she could walk over to the next gully. The elder man seemed to think about it for a moment.

Victoria smiled at the young man, and he smiled back. He was a tall, good-looking lad with perfect posture, good teeth and a beautiful smile. His golden hair was longish, but he appeared clean. His father glanced at him in time to see his son's smile.

"Ah, don't be fallin' for the enemy, Dirk, or your mother will want to know why."

Dirk blushed from one ear to the other, but he smiled and lowered his eyes from Victoria's gaze.

His father looked back at the rest of the group, all of

whom appeared to be sleeping, some flat on the ground with their hats over their faces, others under the shade of the bushes.

"Go on, then," he said motioning to Victoria with a wave. "And see you're back quickly."

Victoria nodded, and both men turned to walk back to where they had been. She hastened across the hard-packed sand to a small indentation in the terrain that placed her below the line of sight of the men. She pulled out her leather case and chose two of the mirrors. She lay down with the sun to her back. She caught the sun with the second mirror, which was reflected in the first mirror, and pointed at the approaching cloudbank. She had nothing to create a shutter effect, so she flicked her wrist quickly, as a shutter might, to cut the transmission of the light flashes. Angling the mirror just right to catch the rays of the dwindling sun, she set about to save the Empire. Here's hoping someone sees the flashes!

Short, Long
Long, Long
A-M-
Long, Short, Short, Short
B-
"What's taking so long?" the Boer shouted.

"Be right there," Victoria called out. I need to abbreviate this code.

Short, Short, Long
Short, Short, Short
U-S-
Short

H is four shorts, so maybe they'll figure out the last one is both an S and an H. Well, taking poetic license, of course.

Victoria shoved her mirrors into the case and pocketed it. She scrambled across the sand and sprinted up over the sand dune to the sight of seven men standing with their rifles trained on her.

THIRTY

"I'm sorry. So sorry..." she said. She tried to catch her breath. Her voice was hoarse. "There were scorpions...very close to my...to my...very close," she stuttered, her face reddening. She lowered her eyes and prepared to die.

She heard the laughter first, then looked up to see the rifles lowered. She breathed a sigh hearing hearty guffaws as the Boer men no doubt conjured up the thought of her lily white bum coming perilously close to a stinger.

"But you are not hurt?" the English-speaking man's son inquired. He was not smiling.

Victoria focused all her attention on him. She shook her head in negation, then smiled at him. The others backed away and showed great interest in their boots.

"My name is Dirk," he said approaching her.

"Victoria," she answered. Extending her hand, she was unsure if this was the proper gesture between a Boer and his enemy. But he took her hand and held it.

"I am sorry we must hold you here. My father is against it, but the other man, Hans, insists."

"Is Hans the leader," she asked.

Dirk shook his head. "No, the leader is my father, but he is a fair man, a just man, and he tries to give his men some leeway."

Dirk looked back at the others.

"Hans is quite bitter, though. He has lost his entire family--wife, two sons, brother and parents. He has only a sister-in-law and her children left, his brother's children, at the camp."

Victoria nodded. "And your family?" she asked. "Do you know if they are well?"

"They are being held in a prison camp. In Port Elizabeth." His tone was flat and dispirited. Again, he glanced at back at the others.

"We had some thought of sneaking into the camp soon, so we left our unit and came this direction. But we know they've got some ships unloading, so we're going back the way we came," Dirk said. "Soon as the sun goes down."

Victoria swallowed. So they weren't planning to ambush anyone. Six Boers could take on 200 British troops or more and had done so throughout the conflict. But these men were trying to see their loved ones. She thought about her own discoveries at the camp, and wondered at the rage and revenge these six Boers might take if they saw the conditions in the camp at Port Elizabeth.

"Which way did you come?" she asked.

"Right across this section of desert," he said, frowning as he looked to the east and contemplated a return trip across the inhospitable terrain. "I guess we're going to leave you here. With some water."

"Oh."

He shuffled in place and looked in the direction of Port Elizabeth. "Got to be some troops coming down that highway by tomorrow," he said. "Maybe even tonight."

"How can you be sure?" She didn't think he'd answer a question like that.

"Intelligence told us they landed three days ago. Got to be on the road soon."

He was guileless. She liked him for that. She liked everything she had observed about him. Something steady and dependable about him. She looked toward Port Elizabeth. Her motorbike was broken and bent, she had the clothes she was wearing and the thought of spending the night alone in this desert did not appeal. Her concerns were reflected in her frown.

"I'm sorry," Dirk said. "If it was up to me..."

Her body relaxed and her voice softened. "What would you do?" she asked.

"I'd stay and protect you. That is, I'd keep you company. I'm sure you can protect yourself."

"Not without a weapon."

He looked up with a start. "You're right. I hadn't thought."

They looked at one another and Victoria could see the light of compassion and affection in his eyes. He was a handsome young man. And kind, she thought.

"I'll leave you my knife," he said, unbuckling the holder from his belt.

"No, I couldn't!" she said.

"You can return it to me, later...when next we meet."

Victoria shrugged and nodded her ascent. "Did you learn English here in Africa?"

154

Dirk smiled. "No, in Frankfort. We arrived four years ago. My grandparents are Dutch."

"My cousin is German," she blurted out.

"Your cousin?" he repeated. "Where in Germany does he live?"

Victoria had to think. "Potsdam?"

Dirk grinned. "Perhaps you'll also be telling me you are the Kaiser's cousin, then," he said.

Dormier's eyes widened. "Why ever would you say that?"

Dirk laughed. His features softened. "I like you, Victoria. You have a wonderful sense of humor. Perhaps when this terrible war is over...?"

Victoria blinked. "I would like to know you better, too, Dirk," she said. *Oh, Lord, Jack. What have you got me into?*

Dirk handed her the knife sheath and watched as she attached it to her belt. She looked up. He said nothing but gazed at her with such an intensity she blushed. But she did not look away.

"Tot ons weer ontmoet," he whispered.

Until we meet again.

THIRTY ONE

Victoria waited in the pitch black night, scanning the sky in the hopes of seeing some headlights coming from the direction of Port Elizabeth. Just before the sun set, she found a small hillock alongside the highway that would hide her from an oncoming enemy while leaving her close enough to hail a ride from British soldiers. She thought it must be around ten, almost 24 hours since she took a tumble on the bike and landed right in the enemy's lap. She took a sip of the water they had left her and swished the canteen around enough to know she hadn't much water left. She was also hungry, but the hardtack in her pocket seemed too awful to contemplate; she'd have to get far hungrier to tackle it.

Victoria was looking skyward, her back against a small boulder, her legs stretched out before her, when she heard it. Slowly and silently she brought her knees up to her chest and sat very still. It could be animal or human, but it was getting close. Something was traveling alongside the road, in the ditch on the other side of the hill that hid her. It sounded like someone dragging something behind him. Then she heard it, the guttural sound of Afrikaans being spoken. The voice sounded familiar.

"Dit is waar ons het haar verlaat, maar waar is sy nou?"

This is where we left her, but where is she now?

It was Hans! Victoria sank her head and shoulders as low as she could without changing position. She heard a low groan, the growl of intense pain. He was dragging someone on a makeshift sling.

"Nie meer nie! Geen verdere! Laat my hier!"

No more! No further! Leave me here!

It was Dirk. Victoria heard Hans mumble, but he stopped dragging the sling. Something must have happened. Dirk sounded like he was dying. She heard Hans shuffle the sling a couple more feet until he placed the person on the side of the small hill she hid behind. They couldn't have been four feet from her. She leaned into the boulder, trying to hide in its shadow. She heard more shuffling as Hans tried to position Dirk with his back against the hill.

"As sy in die omgewing is, sal sy vind, en waarskynlik jou doodmaak. Maar as jy wil. Sterkte!"

If she's in the area, she will find you and probably kill you. But as you wish. Good luck!

Victoria heard Dirk moan, but Hans began walking back in the direction from whence he came, which was in the direction of Port Elizabeth. She tried to imagine what had happened. Where was Dirk's father? The other men? She sat perfectly still for nearly a quarter hour, long past when she could hear Hans walking. Dirk made a few low moans but seemed to have fallen asleep. Finally, her legs screamed to be moved. With as much stealth as she could manage, she stood up.

"Wie is dit? Victoria?"

She made a quick decision.

"Yes, Dirk, it is Victoria."

She moved in his direction but could only see a large lump up against the side of the hill. As her eyes adjusted, the moonlight clarified the unimaginable. It was Dirk with both his legs missing, his face bloodied almost beyond recognition and the pain and fright in his eyes more than she could bear to see. She crawled over to him.

"Dirk...oh Dirk, what happened?"

"We were ourselves ambushed, Victoria. My father escaped, I think. Two of the men died. Hans was wounded, but not too badly. He volunteered to bring me back here."

"Why here, Dirk?" Victoria's hands shook as she pulled the tarp around him tighter. He was shivering. She removed her jacket and laid it across his chest. She wrapped the arms of the jacket around the back of him. She almost fainted at the sight of his bloodied stumps.

"I'm going to die, I'm afraid, Victoria. I'm sorry."

She choked back a cry. "No, you're not. You can't!"

"Look at me, Victoria. This is what your country has left me as, a half- dead man with less than half a future. If I don't die, I'm sure I'll wish I had."

Victoria murmured, "Let me keep you warm." She scooted up next to him and placed her arm around his shoulders. He leaned his head back on her arm and looked feverishly up at the sky.

She took her crystal out of her pants pocket. She held it over his head, even touched it to the back of his neck.

He seemed not to notice. Everything she knew to do she forgot. She forgot what her mother's note said. She forgot how to pull the power from the crystal. How could the Magick fail her now? His voice stopped her from further thought.

"I love the stars," he whispered. "I think I see one I will name Victoria."

She looked at him and closed her eyes. She replaced the crystal into her pant leg pocket and picked up her canteen. With care, she placed it against his lips, and though he whetted them, he did not drink.

"Drink, dear Dirk, please drink!"

He shook his head. "Do you know what I wish for?"

"What? What would you wish?" She pulled him closer as his trembling seemed to increase.

"I wish for a kiss."

"A...kiss?"

"I've never been kissed by a girl, Victoria."

Victoria bit her lip. *And yet, I have...been kissed by a girl.*

"I know someone must be waiting at home for you," he labored. "But if we, as friends...perhaps..."

"I will happily kiss you, Dirk." She moved her arm slightly and turned her head to face him. He didn't immediately turn to her. He looked up at the stars for a long time. He was so quiet, she wondered what he was thinking.

She turned her gaze to the stars. She wondered which one was Victoria. Softly she began to whisper to him.

"And when I kiss you, I think the stars you are looking at will wink at you. They will say, 'Ah, good, Dirk has a new friend. Victoria is his friend.'"

She turned to him, but her smile froze in place until it

159

melted into a grimace of sorrow. His eyes were open, but his life was gone.

"Nee, nee, nee! No, no, no!"

When he didn't move, she took her fingers and closed his eyes. Her palm lingered on his skin, his cheek so hot and feverish a few seconds ago, now cool to her touch.

Death was so full. All of a person was gone.

It didn't matter what he knew or didn't know about her, he would never know now. It didn't matter that despite their brief encounter, she was genuinely fond of him. She respected him. He didn't know that. It didn't matter how much she appreciated his offer of friendship. He would never know.

She looked up at the stars, and her eyes scanned the black depths in a futile search for the star he had seen. She would never find it. She would never find Victoria. She would never know which star he chose. A sentence from her mother's instructions came back to her now. *Never use the power to gain what you want for someone who loves you if you do not love the same in return.* She tried to repeat it aloud so as not to forget again...never use the power to gain...She choked on the words, her tears strangling her voice. Weeping inconsolably, her heart cursed the ruins and madness of war as she turned and kissed him gently on the lips, just as he had wished for. She could give him that. She could give him a small part of the Victoria she had found.

THIRTY TWO

Victoria made it back to Field Hospital 8, after hitching a ride with a mounted horse unit heading for the hospital with supplies. In her absence, 12 boxcars of patients had been unloaded and transferred to the various wards. Soldiers requiring immediate surgery, usually those with missing or mangled limbs, or organ wounds, were transported first. Some of them, having survived the anxious, grueling, overheated dark hell of the boxcar, expired upon arrival or from the rough jostling of exhausted soldiers trying to save lives.

She saw Colonel Parker alone in his office at one end of the Administration tent. He held his head in his hands and looked as though he were sleeping. But he raised one hand and slowly tousled his hair. She could see it was damp with perspiration, as was his shirt. His jacket was

161

placed neatly across the desk. She waited until he looked up and saluted. He waved her forward.

"Where the hell have you been, Dormier?" he asked. "I know you've been Absent Without Leave for two days. What I don't know is: Why?"

"Sir, I was captured by the enemy on the road back from Port Elizabeth, sir."

"Oh well, hell, why didn't you just say so. How many? Get a description? My God, you weren't...you weren't hurt were you?"

"No, sir, I was not."

"I can't think to tell you what a relief that is, Private."

"Yes, sir. Thank you, sir." *No shit, Colonel.*

"What in blazes was the enemy doing that close to the port? How many were there?"

"Seven, sir. They were...I think they became lost from their contingent, sir. But they did not hurt me in any manner."

"What happened to them? You kill 'em all?" he asked, laughing.

Victoria was startled. "Oh, no, sir! I mean, I had no weapon, sir."

"Where did you get that knife, Private?"

Victoria touched her belt. "I found it on the ground, sir, after they left. One of them must have left it."

Parker stared at her for a moment, then nodded. "Smart of you to let the troops know they were in for an ambush, Private. Didn't realize you were in possession of heliograph instrumentation." It was a question posing as a statement.

"Well, sir, yes, stroke of luck that. Actually the Boers had a heliograph with them, and I managed to use it while they slept."

"So they were reconnaissance, then! They've probably already transmitted intelligence about our troop movement from the port."

Victoria stood there motionless. And expressionless.

"Don't you think, Private? You quite allright, Dormier? You look a little peaked."

"I'm...fine, Colonel, thank you. And I agree, Colonel. They've probably done just that, although I didn't see them use the heliograph while I was present."

"Hmm. Can't think why else they'd be in that particular area...but I suppose it's possible they don't know. Best to assume they did though," he said, standing up quickly. "I'll be sending this information to Baden-Powell. He'd want to know. Thank you, Private. You've performed admirably. If you weren't departing, I'd promote you!"

"Well, sir, since I apparently must depart, would it be possible for me to do so at a higher rank?" Victoria shrugged. "You know, sir, just to show my...my family that I accomplished something?"

"Let me think about that," Parker said. "Good night young lady...uh, Private."

Victoria saluted. "Good night, sir, I hope you get some rest."

He walked past her mumbling. "Bloody not bloody likely."

Victoria exhaled. That was close. Too close. She wondered if what she had done could be considered treason, but she concluded not. She looked around and realized that Colonel Parker had dimmed the gaslight on his desk. His entire office was bathed in the shadows of quarter light from the other areas of the tent. She walked over to his desk and saw several sheaves of blank paper laid neatly under the Colonel's writing instrument. She looked around again, and then sat down at the desk. No one walking the fabric- walled corridors of the tent could see her, but she had a full view of the various activities farther out in the tent. A few nurses and aides de camp were seated at desks preparing reports. She picked up a pen.

Dearest Auntie,

As I have come down to Africa to assist, in whatever meager way I can, the effort to secure Your Majesty's benevolent Empire, I have, nonetheless, come upon some information that I believe you will find most unpleasant and unsavory. Certainly, this information must not be connected, in any way or words, to Your Majesty's goals, values and character. I know that you have sent for me...and, of course, your wish is my command.

If, however, you wish me to expound upon this travesty, please send me a communication by return. And perhaps you could ask Colonel Parker to delay my departure for another week; I wish to obtain a couple more pieces of evidence with regard to this most important and astounding discovery I have made. Additionally, I made contact with Mr. Pierce, and although our meeting was...Fruitful? Delicious? Interrupted? ...promising, he's...where the dickens is he? ...off on a short mission at the moment, though I have reason to believe he is nearby. Please advise as to your hopeful agreement that I may stay a while longer to accomplish all my goals on your behalf. I hope my Auntie's health is improving, as I pray for you each evening and hope that God favors me with my request for your long life.

With love, fondness and adoration, your loyal niece, who is blessed and honored to have been named for you, Victoria D.

THIRTY THREE

Alice made it to the back of the latrine shed without being seen, but she crouched down next to her bike for nearly 15 minutes in case another Boer materialized. Just as she was about to stand, she heard a rustle of leaves and voices. She peeked through the spokes of her tyres and frowned. The same man who had left the latrine a while ago was coming back toward it with another man. The tall man was gesturing with his hands in front of him as though trying to describe—handlebars! They're coming for the bike!

Alice crawled behind a nearby high bush just as they approached the side of the outhouse. She could see them clearly. They were so close she could smell them. They stood murmuring about the bike. How long would it be before they saw her? The second man began to roll the bike out from behind the latrine and the tall man followed. Straddling the bike, the first man got it started.

He motioned for the tall man to hop on the back, but the man demurred. The rider laughed, and the tall man scowled. Finally, he turned off the bike and set it down on its side. They talked between themselves for a while, and then headed back into the bushes from whence they came. Again, Alice waited. Longer this time. Someone might have heard the bike's roar. Someone might, even now, be watching the bike from the same kind of bushes in which she hid.

After about an hour, Alice's legs began to cramp up and she needed to move around. She crept out from behind the bushes, and after looking all around, crept quickly to her bike. She righted it and began to roll it in the direction of the main road. Once there, she pulled over into the brush again and sat quietly for a while. She mentally prepared herself for the mile ride to the front. She knew it was to be set up a half mile west of the earlier frontlines with wide flanks. If she didn't get shot at by the Boers, she could easily be shot at by her own. She took a big square handkerchief from an inside pocket of her pants and looked around for a stick. To hell with that! Too hard to ride holding a white flag on a stick. She'd just wave the thing and hope it worked.

Alice walked deeper into the bush and gathered up twigs and small pieces of wood. When she had an armful, she placed three small bundles at various points behind her. She walked to the farthest bundle and struck a match. She walked quicker to the second bundle and did the same thing. She ran to the third bundle of kindling, threw a match on it and took off running hard for her bike. She rolled it out onto the road, jumped on the gas pedal and watched as nothing happened. She tried to kick it in again. Already the woods behind her were smoking and crackling with the fires she started.

Christ! Did I flood it? She rolled the bike another 50 feet, gave it a good talking to and jumped the pedal again. With some heart-stopping sputtering, it started up, and she jumped onto it so fast she almost threw it over. She stepped on the gas and headed down the first road. She glanced back and the whole area behind her was in flames. To her right, in the distance, she heard the pop of a Mauser. Then a second shot. Then a third. A Boer was somewhere off to her right and getting closer. At the sound of the fourth shot and the ping as it hit her handlebars, she realized she wasn't escaping the marksman, she was heading toward him. Seconds later she slowed the cycle at the sight of four Boer guerillas forming a human firing squad across the road up ahead.

With more bravado than she felt, she gunned the cycle again and drove right at the line. Surprised at her move, they scattered to either side of the road giving her just enough time to drive beyond their range. But she knew they were good marksmen, so she leaned in tight and low, her body hugging the body of the machine. She got the bike up to its top speed and saw the faint glow of campfires up ahead. *The British! Finally.* She pulled the handkerchief out of her pocket and began waving it as if her life depended on the motion. And it did. A forward section of infantrymen met her on the open veldt, and as she skidded to a stop, they lowered their rifles. The corporal in charge demanded her to dismount and move forward with her arms up. She did as she was told, and when he could see her uniform and rank, he saluted. Unfortunately, the adrenaline that got Jack Pierce to his safe harbor dissipated in full-body relief, and Alice Ponsonby passed out in front of 25 men.

168

THIRTY FOUR

St. James was surprised to see a stretcher headed for her tent. No shots had been fired as far as she knew. The bearers deposited Alice in the Infirmary and rushed back out of the tent after giving a brief rendition of what happened.

St. James set about to remove the officer's jacket and loosen his shirt. She took a reading of his pulse and pulled up his eyelids. He was definitely unconscious. St. James called her orderly over.

"Let's get this officer undressed, soldier. I need to check for broken bones, injuries."

St. James returned to her desk to begin filling out a short admittance report. There might not be time for this later, but, for now, she'd proceed according to protocol.

"Ma'am?"

St. James looked up. "What is it?"

169

The orderly just stared at her. Then he vaguely motioned in the direction of the supine officer. "There's something I think you should see, ma'am."

St. James got up and walked over to the patient. The orderly had removed the officer's shirt. He had a tight bandage wrapped around his chest.

"Is it a wound?" she asked reaching for the edge of the white wrapping.

"I don't know," he said. "I don't see any blood."

"Could be broken ribs, maybe a chest bruise." St. James reached under the dressing with her fingers, then stopped abruptly. She looked the officer up and down from his knees to his throat, then his face. Lovely long eyelashes. "Listen, Jed, I'd kill for a hot cup of tea...I can handle this if you'd go get me one next door in the officer's mess. I'd owe you something special, like some extra tobacco?"

"Right away, ma'am."

As soon as he was out of the tent, St. James pulled the dressing away from the soldier's chest and put her hand inside it. What she felt was a woman's breast. She reached to the other side and felt another breast. She peered over the top of the bandage and confirmed what her hand had told her. St. James starred at the soldier in disbelief. She snapped her head to the side and quickly reached down inside the soldier's pants.

When Jed walked back into the tent, he almost dropped the tea tray at the sound of "Oh fuck."

***

"I will need your real name, of course."
"Of course. Alice Jane Ponsonby."

170

"Would you like to contact anyone? At home, I mean?" St. James avoided eye contact with the patient until not hearing an answer forced her to look up.

"You won't believe it," Alice stated matter-of-factly.

"Oh, try me," St James answered, a small flicker of a smile feathering the corners of her mouth.

"Well, the Queen, of course. Her Majesty will want to know I'm here."

"Of course," answered St. James. Turning back toward her desk, she added, "I'll get on it."

"No, I'm quite serious," Alice said to her back. "If not the Queen, then her daughter, Princess Helena."

St. James turned to look at Alice. "Anyone else you'd like us to contact?"

Alice thought about it. "Well, of course, you probably know Victoria Dormier, the Queen's niece? She's here somewhere. In fact, I'm looking for her so as to return with her to England as soon as possible."

St. James laughed out loud. She laughed so hard she had to hold her sides. She doubled over laughing. When she stopped, she had to dry her cheeks from the tears of laughter.

Alice looked at her questioningly. "I do hope you'll help me."

"As appealing as it sounds," St. James said before getting into another fit of uncontrollable laughter. "Oh." She cleared her throat. "As appealing as it sounds, Miss...Miss Ponsonby, I'm afraid I must report this, this most exceptional turn of events to my immediate superior. Captain Rosemary Privet."

"Oh! Wonderful," said Alice. "She knows me! I was just speaking to her this morning! Lucky turn, that, say?"

St. James smiled. "Lucky? That depends. Were you

speaking to her as Captain Jack Pierce or as Alice Ponsonby?"

The smile on Alice's face faded. "It's Lady Alice, actually, Lieutenant."

"Of course," said St. James. "It would almost have to be, now wouldn't it!" She began to whistle softly.

"Are you quite all right, Lieutenant?"

"Not really, Lady Jack, but I figure I'm in a bit better shape than you at the moment. Let me go send a message to Captain Privet."

"Thank you. Will you be sure to add the part about Her Majesty...or at least Dormier? I'm most...I'm quite...I'm concerned about Victoria."

"Which one?"

"Oh! Dormier of course," said Alice. "She's...a friend. A close friend."

"I wouldn't leave it out for all the tea in England," St. James said.

THIRTY FIVE

St. James finished up the communication about Ponsonby, reread it, sealed it and asked Jed to deliver it immediately to Captain Privet at Hospital Camp.

"I'd have to be gone about a half hour," he said. "I'll send an infantry guard back to stand at the tent."

"Oh, is that really necessary?" St James asked.

"Standard procedure ma'am for all medical tents. We're within a quarter miles of the front ma'am."

"Right. Then off you go, Jed. Get whomever you find to stand guard."

St. James took a large swallow of her lukewarm coffee. Glancing at Ponsonby, who had her eyes closed, St. James smiled. She actually did believe the woman. She wondered what the connection between her and Dormier was, but she surmised there must be one.

St. James heard a rustling outside the tent flap and

stood up. Before she could take a step, three heavily armed Boer guerilla fighters, burst in. One of them was bleeding heavily from a wound in his upper arm.

Ponsonby opened her eyes.

"We need you to help him," one of them said in perfect English.

Without skipping a beat, St. James pointed to the bed next to Alice. "I don't have a medic here right now," the doctor said, "and I'm guessing he needs surgery, but I'll do what I can."

Two of the men stood on either side of the tent flap, their weapons at the ready.

St. James ripped off the man's jacket and shirt. He was bleeding badly. She stanched the blood and cleaned the wound, which did not appear to be from a gunshot.

"What happened to him?" she asked the other two.

"Does it matter?"

"It could," she said. "The skin tore very jaggedly."

"He was trying to climb over a barbed wire fence, and...and he injured himself."

St. James paused almost imperceptibly, then leaned into the patient and peered into the open wound. "I think I can close this wound," she said. "But if it's infected, it will cause further damage, possibly to his organs."

"He has to be able to move."

St. James shrugged lightly and set about to repair the wounded man.

Alice watched through half-open lids. She was more interested in the two at the tent flap. They must have sneaked in before the new guard arrived—if he arrived. Odd that he hadn't come inside the tent to announce his presence. Alice considered that he could be lying unconscious, or worse, in the bush by now. She wondered what the presence of these three meant about the position of the bigger enemy forces. She moved her head slightly as moaning came from the bed where Dr. St. James was working.

"What is this soldier's wounds?" one of the men asked, indicating Alice.

St. James looked up and then over at Alice. "He just got the wind knocked out of him," she said. "He'll be fine in a while."

The two men looked at Alice and she at them.

"There, there, this will make you feel better," St. James said to the man. He winced as she shot a syringe of morphine into his thigh. Within moments he became quiet, his breathing less jagged, his pain less intense.

They all heard the commotion outside and the gunshots in the distance. St. James turned to the two men near the front of the tent. "It won't be long before I begin getting patients. If you're going to move him, it should be soon."

The men nodded and conferred. Finally, one stepped forward.

"We cannot travel with him, but we fear for his life with your soldiers."

St. James nodded. She understood their concern. She had heard the stories. Captured Boers were not well-treated, and injured ones were treated worse.

"So we will take your soldier here," he said, pointing to Alice. "As insurance that a fair trade can be made when our man recovers."

THIRTY SIX

St. James got the wounded Boer up and walking around the Infirmary. He was still dazed, but reasonably coherent.

"My son," he said. "I've got to find my son."

"Where did you leave him?" asked St. James, reaching to steady him when he began to tilt. They walked around the room, and he gathered his strength.

"We were in Port Elizabeth," he said. "My wife..."

St. James swallowed hard as she saw the rims of his eyelids redden. He coughed a couple times.

"My wife is in one of the concentrated camps, and my daughter. Three of us, me, my son and one of the men who brought me here got over the fence, but we were spotted. When the guards began shooting I had to make a run for it. I stumbled and got cut by the barbed fence, but my wife saw me. I know she did—she called my name. And my son...I must find him."

"Where did you last see him?" St. James asked. She glanced anxiously at the tent flap, worried that any second someone from her side would walk in.

"He was with one of my men. They took off in a different direction. We lost them. So we came this direction because I needed help. But we couldn't make it to our regiment. We couldn't find it," he clarified.

St. James doubted that last bit, but she let it slide. Something about this man affected her. He was just someone's father, someone's husband, someone's son. His English was perfect, but he spoke with an accent that seemed both Dutch and German.

As she directed him back to the cot, she heard a woman's voice. With typical gusto, Rosemary Privet entered the Infirmary tent.

"Doesn't look like a woman," she said, removing her gloves. "I say! What's this?" Privet exclaimed, realizing the man was a Boer.

St. James looked up, alarm shadowing her face as the Boer sat down heavily on the bed. "Oh, Lieutenant Pierce isn't here. Come over to my desk Captain, I have something to show you."

Once seated, St. James glanced over to the patient. He was on his back, eyes closed. She could hear him snoring softly. The exercise had worn him out.

Quickly she apprised Privet of the situation. It took some elaboration, but Privet nodded firmly.

"Wouldn't have barged in here like Bonaparte after his first victory if I'd known," Privet said.

St James glanced over at the sleeping patient. "No harm done, I think.

"Anyway, first off, I've got to get this man out of here," said Privet. "He's a prisoner of war now."

St. James nodded. "I understand."

"Secondly, this has to go up much higher than me, St. James. I doubt if even Colonel Parker can authorize a prisoner swap—not to mention we'd be swapping a Boer soldier for...a female British citizen who's been masquerading as a British officer, no less!"

"Right," agreed St. James. "But I did promise her, this Alice Ponsonby, that I'd relay to you the business about contacting Her Majesty, her Majesty's daughter or Dormier."

"I've got a war to help run, here, doctor! Can't be dancing to Dormier's tango, no matter who she is."

"But you will mention that part to Colonel Parker?"

Privet hesitated. "Yes," she said softly, "but only because it's you. You seem to think more highly of this one here than most would," she added inclining her head in the direction of the Boer soldier. "All right, get him on a stretcher and cover him head to toe. I'll arrange to have him taken to Number 8."

"Thank you, Captain," St. James said, holding Privet's gaze. "I do think there's something different about him, though I can't say what. As for Ponsonby...I'd ask Dormier about her if I were you. She seems to...they seem to have a...special friendship."

"What does that mean?" asked Privet, her eyes narrowing.

"I'm not sure. I honestly do not know. It's just a feeling I have."

Privet stood up, shook her head and adjusted her cap. "If I run the rest of my week on your feelings, I'm likely to get court-martialed."

St. James grinned. "Oh, I imagine you could run on your own feelings and get the same result."

The color rose in Privet's cheeks and St. James pretended not to notice as they both turned toward the patient.

Together they lifted the Boer onto a gurney, covered him up and tucked him in tight. "Don't say a word to anyone," St. James whispered to him. "Pretend you're unconscious. We're taking you to hospital, but if you want to get there alive, heed my words."

"You're a kind woman," he whispered back. He closed his eyes and did not open them until the ambulance arrived at Number 8. The gurney was led into the receiving ward by Rosemary Privet.

***

"Monty, need your girls to get this man's wounds re-dressed, check him for internal injuries and set him up in the small room at the end of the ward." Privet marched into the room swatting at the tiny flying gnats that seemed to be everywhere on the veldt.

The nurses blinked. The small room was for the highest ranking officers with the most severe wounds. "And after you'd had a chance to check him over yourself, could you meet me in Colonel Parker's office?"

"Sounds serious, Captain."

"Oh, you have no idea," said Privet leaning in to speak to her confidentially.

"You going to give me a hint?"

Privet took a deep breath. "Well, Monty, if you thought the Queen's niece was a handful, what do you think of a Boer soldier being exchanged for a British lieutenant who is actually a woman? And who is, I have it on good authority, quite fond of our Dormier in ways that

179

could be as easily praised as damned—could either launch a ship or drown a nation."

Montgomery's face went blank. Slowly her eyebrows rose a fraction, her dimples creased just enough to suggest a smile. Or a smirk. "Right. Well, if that ship has indeed left the port, Rosemary, there's precious little we can do about it. Even singing 'God Save the Queen' seems somehow inadequate. Love the notion of St. Bitch dealing with that one, though!"

Rosie snuffed a laugh and headed for Colonel Parker's office.

THIRTY SEVEN

It didn't take long for Colonel Parker to grasp the implications of Alice Ponsonby as Jack Pierce once the Queen's telegram arrived.

"From: The Queen To: Colonel Parker. Return Lieutenant Jack Pierce and Victoria Dormier to England immediately. Stop. Acknowledge receipt and indicate Ship Name and Departure date. Stop."

"Get Dormier in here," Parker said to an aid. "And have Dr. Montgomery join us as soon as she's able."

Parker and Privet sat tensely before one another.

"Most annoying," Parker ventured. "Trying to fight a goddamn war and all the Queen's relatives are getting in my way. Wouldn't matter so much were it not for the fact that it's Her Majesty's bloody war I'm talking about."

Privet listened but made sure she nodded neither assent nor dissent.

181

"We have one chance to put this right in the next 24 hours," Privet offered.

"That's putting my window of response time to Her Majesty at the outside limit," Parker said. He lit a cigarette, only to notice he had one going already.

"Captain," he said, offering her the newly lit one, "Will you join me?"

Privet accepted the tobacco smoothly, neither of them letting on the gesture was anything more, or less, than a fully intended courtesy. They puffed in silence, then Parker made a display of rearranging some items on his desk, coughed a couple times lightly and gave Privet a nervous smile.

"If what I'm to understand about Dormier and this...this Ponsonby girl—say! You don't suppose she's related to the Earl? By golly she must be!" he said, answering his own question.

"That I wouldn't know, sir. But Dormier would."

"Which?" he said.

"Either," said Privet, her face neutral.

"Right, well, I suppose I'm far more concerned with who she is than what she is," he said.

Having got the sticky wicket out of the way, by minimizing it to the lower levels of unimportance, Parker looked off into space.

"We'll have to do a trade somehow," he mused.

At that moment, Private Dormier and Montgomery were announced. Both entered and saluted.

"At ease, please have a seat," said Parker. "How's the patient, doctor?"

"Good," Montgomery said, accepting the cigarette he offered across the desk. He did not offer one to Victoria. "I think we've avoided gangrene, so that'll save the arm. His fever is down a notch, but he's in and out of full consciousness."

They all sat quietly. Finally, Parker turned to Victoria. "Private, who is this Alice Ponsonby?"

"A friend of my family, sir."

"The Earl's daughter, then."

"Granddaughter, sir."

Parker nodded. "I know him. Surprised I've not heard from him by now. Although Her Majesty's wire does trump any and all, sent or unsent."

Victoria's eyes widened.

Parker continued. "Your...Her Majesty wants you both sent home immediately. There's only one big problem: The Boers have Alice Ponsonby as a prisoner—insurance to see they get their man back. Trouble is, I've got 24 hours, at the outside, to wire the Queen with the name of the ship you'll both be on and the departure and arrival date."

Victoria lowered her gaze to her lap. "I see."

"Monty," Parker said, smiling and using the familiar address to set her at ease. "Have we any idea where this prisoner exchange is to take place?"

"None, sir, and I was so, so confounded by the entire situation, I'm afraid I neglected to ask."

"Understandable," offered Parker. "Well, if this Dirk fellow can talk, maybe—

Victoria looked up. "Sir? I beg your pardon, sir, but I might know him."

"Know him, Dormier? How could you possibly know him?" Parker's neck was getting red.

"When I was captured, sir. One of the men was called 'Dirk.'

"It's a fairly common name among the Boers," said

Monty drily.

"Yes, actually there are two of them called that, father and son. I just thought...well, I wondered if I...might I see the man, sir?"

Parker looked at Privet and Montgomery. They both shrugged.

"Can't see as how it could hurt," he finally said. "But whether he is or isn't the man who captured you, try to find out how the devil we're meant to get word to his men for an exchange! Dismissed, private! Monty, take Dormier to the patient, will you?"

Victoria and Monty both stood. "Certainly, Sir." Saluting in unison, they turned and left the room.

"What do you make of this, Privet?" asked Parker.

"I don't know, sir," she said.

"Oh, come on, woman, you and me, we go way back. I know you and you know me. What's the relationship there, between this Jack Pierce, uh, this Ponsonby and Dormier?"

"I'd have to say it sounds intimate, Colonel."

"Quite right, that's what I think. Right, well, so what are my odds?"

"Sir?"

"What are the odds I get the exchange done within 24 hours?"

Privet thought for a moment. "About 70/30, sir."

"In which direction? Goddamn, Privet don't be so obtuse!"

"You've got a 70 percent chance of meeting your deadline if they're lovers, and a 30 percent chance of not meeting your deadline if they're lovers. Sir," she added.

"That's not too bad. But what if they're not, uh, you, uh quite...that?"

"If they're not lovers, sir, you've got zero chance. No mutual incentive."

Parker thought about it a moment. "Well, goddamn it, Privet, go find out! Ask Dormier!"

Privet rose. "Did you want me to report back immediately, sir?"

"Only if my military career is as good as over, Privet. Otherwise, I'll assume that Jack Pierce, Alice Ponsonby and Victoria Dormier are the only ménage à trois in British military history to be a...a couple."

"Yes, sir."

THIRTY EIGHT

The minute Victoria saw Dirk's father lying on a gurney, she rushed toward him. He opened his eyes, then smiled.

"Hello, Private," he said.

"Sir, hello..."

"My son went with Hans...not sure where. Need to see Dirk, Private."

As she looked into his worried eyes, she saw his son's eyes looking back at her. Hooded by fevered and swollen lids, his eyes sought her out as his son's had. A million thoughts collided in her brain. But one began creeping into her awareness, then shot up like molten magma through the volcanic cacophony in her mind.

"I might be able to help, sir." She reached over to touch his arm. His free hand moved to cover her hand and hold it tight against his arm. "But first you need to rest a bit, recover some more."

He nodded and closed his eyes. Victoria looked up and saw Monty staring at her expectantly.

Victoria bent down toward Dirk. "Sir, where should we meet up with your men to exchange you with Lieutenant Pierce?"

He lay perfectly still for many seconds, and she pulled back a bit, thinking he had drifted off to sleep.

"Right where we met you," he said. "That's where Hans and Dirk were headed when we got out of Port Elizabeth. We split up when we got to the camp, but we all agreed to meet within 48 hours. They don't know I was cut by the fence. They will be expecting me in...the next 12 hours I think. If I don't come, they will leave for...for another location." His eyes remained closed.

Victoria's face blanched. Dirk didn't seem to have known the extent of his son's wounds when they separated. Hans would see the cross. Maybe. Would he figure it out? Maybe not. Then, Dirk the father would see it when they traded him for Jack. She was going to have to tell him before the prisoner exchange.

"All right, sir, then rest, so we can transport you. Another couple hours and you will be on the mend."

"I need a horse," he added. "I need to be able to ride it."

Montgomery motioned for Victoria to follow her to a small office area on the opposite side of the tent. They kept their voices low.

"There's no way on earth that man will be ready to ride a horse," Monty declared.

Victoria looked at the physician. Monty looked back. They sat there like that until Monty sighed.

"Your shoulder wound," she said matter-of-factly. "That cleared up miraculously fast. Too fast."

Victoria nodded but said nothing.

"So, Dormier, are you proposing to get this man up and capable of riding a horse in...in the same way?"

Victoria nodded again. "There are no guarantees," she said.

"Right, well there never is with that conjuring stuff, or whatever it is."

Victoria laughed. "Not quite conjuring," she said but explained no further. "I'll need to be alone with him for a few minutes. For a while."

Without another word, Monty stood and gestured toward the opposite side of the tent. "Give me a moment to let the guards know you have permission."

Victoria stood where she had been left until she saw Monty wave her forward. The guards stepped aside and Dormier stepped in.

Dirk was sleeping and did not rouse as she approached him. Kneeling down alongside his bed, Victoria pulled out her leather case and extracted the crystal. She warmed it with her hands, turned it several times, and placed it against Dirk's skin. His left arm lay alongside his body. She wasn't sure if it had to be right on the wound, but that was pretty impossible so she got it as close to the wound as possible. She closed her eyes and brought her mother's handwritten note to her inner sight. Eight steps? She had only used six on her own wound.

She proceeded through each of the directions her mother had written. After reviewing the steps, she sat in perfect stillness as her blind eyes imagined the wound, the torn and angry skin, the stitches, the color of the mercurochrome, the dressing over the wound. Then she went the other direction. She worked her way up from inside the wound, her eyes moving silently through flesh and blood and...was that pus? It was. She lingered there until any yellow liquid oozing from his wound disappeared, and then she worked her way around the entry of the wound, seeing the skin mending itself, seeing the scar tissue become little more than a thin line. After exiting the wound, she bent her head in supplication, or exhaustion.

She understood. There was no good war. Her auntie's Empire would win because the brute force of weapons, of wire barricades and wounded spirits, would forestall defeat. But she understood, at that moment, that all empires throughout history had fallen—all of them—and her auntie's Empire eventually would face bigger adversaries, frightening dangers and crushing defeats. And all the diamonds and natural resources of this African continent would not prevent it. All the deaths here would beget far more in the future. She understood that she had no power to change the course of history, but she could try to heal some of the damages, one person at a time.

Would it mean anything in the larger scheme of things? Maybe. Maybe not. She had come to Africa in pursuit of Jack Pierce. But she would leave in the company of Alice Ponsonby. First you save the ones you love; then you save the ones you don't. Sometimes your heart will break. And it will feel as though you will need two hearts.

After a few minutes, she slowly rose and left the room.

THIRTY NINE

By the time the *Princess of Wales* left Port Elizabeth, Victoria found herself in a section of the ship allotted to ladies. There were nurses, medical sisters, ancillary hospital and medic staff like herself and a few British citizens escaping the South African war zones. The rest of the quarters were filled with men in various states of well-being. One section was for soldiers wounded to blindness, amputation and gunshot wounds so serious they were immobilized.

Although a few women seemed to have staterooms of their own, most of the passengers were doubled up in cramped and stuffy quarters below deck. Victoria spent as much time as possible on deck. She needed the air, the wind, even the stormy skies. She looked out at the horizon one evening just as the sun was setting and wondered at her fate. She had missed Jack by four days. He had returned home she was told. She couldn't help but wonder if he had been wounded. She hardly believed he was still alive after the last episode.

She tried to imagine Jack as a woman. It was both difficult and easy, all at once, creating a jumble in her mind that refused to still itself. Alice. Alice. Alice. No. No! She was Jack. She would always be Jack. AliceJack perhaps? Or JackAlice? No. Ridiculous! Just Jack. But her name was really the least of Victoria's concerns, wasn't it? What was she meant to do with a woman? She had never...she never even imagined...well, well she had never, with anyone, come to think of it.

She thought again of Jack's smooth skin, her finely tapered fingers and strong hands. She winced, then blushed, then smiled at the thought of kissing her. She did kiss divinely! *Stop that! Why? She did! She had the most delicious lips, and I loved it when she held me close. Her eyes. Oh, those damn beautiful long eyelashes. I could drown in the pools of light in her eyes, and willingly go to my watery death. Oh, you're the future Queen, allright, queen of drama!*

Victoria wondered, not for the first time, what her Auntie had meant by saying Jack was her secret weapon. How did Auntie even know Jack? True—Auntie knew Mummy's bestie, Lady Ponsonby, so perhaps she had met Jack, er, Alice as Lady Alice. But...when did Alice become Jack? And, and, and! Victoria had so many questions.

When they were three days from England, the end of a fierce storm brought nearly everyone out of their intolerably humid, close quarters and on deck to breathe the rain-cooled air.

Victoria found a small area at the rail hidden from view by walls of equipment. As she leaned on her elbows and looked out to a still moderately turbulent sea, she felt the presence of someone behind her. She felt her body stiffen as a subtle scent of jasmine wafted toward her. She turned around quickly, startling the person behind her.

"Oh!" said Victoria.

"Oh!" said Alice.

They stared at one another for a full beat, and then Alice smiled, the dimple in her left cheek deepening.

"Hello, Treasure."

"Hello, Jack."

Alice smiled. Victoria did not.

"It probably won't do to be calling me that in front of the others," Alice said.

"Oh, I think it's perfect! After all, I met you as Jack, and it's...it's just so hard to come to terms with...Alice."

"I quite understand," Alice said quietly.

"No, actually, you do not," snapped Victoria. "You don't understand at all, but apparently everyone else does!"

"I can explain that part," offered Alice.

"I sincerely doubt it, and most emphatically don't care anyway," Victoria sniffed.

"I see that. And yet..." Alice half turned as if to leave.

"Next you'll be telling me my Auntie instigated this, this match made in hell!"

"This...match?" Alice grinned. "Well, actually, darling, she is aware of it, but no she didn't purposefully throw us together. I met you quite accidentally, remember? When your—oh dear. I'm so sorry about your father. I did hear. I am very sorry. Truly. He was a lovely man."

That's all it took. A split-second later, Victoria was in tears. She sobbed so loudly that Alice reached for her and drew her close. Victoria did not resist. She wept, she keened, she cried so hard she nearly hyper-ventilated.

"Daddy's gone, Jack, and I miss him so..."

192

"Shh, shh, there now," cooed Alice. "My sweet little snorking banbh."

Victoria gurgled at Alice's use of the Gaelic endearment.

"I amth noth your lithel pigleth," she lisped, bleezy eyes blazing through it all.

"No, of course not," soothed Alice as she placed soft, light kisses on Victoria's forehead.

Victoria used Alice's hanky to pat her face, wipe her eyes, and blow her nose. When she finished, she wadded it up and pushed it up inside her sleeve. Alice raised an eyebrow, so Victoria extracted it from her sleeve and...tossed it overboard.

"Hope that wasn't Irish lace," she said, verbally thwacking Alice for her Gaelic comment about little piglets. "And what do you mean Auntie is aware of...it?" asked Victoria. Her voice only quaked a little.

"May I tell you over dinner, Victoria? Please? We could both do with some freshening up, and I have so much to say."

Victoria, hearing her Christian name spoken so gently, relented with a nod. She looked into Alice's eyes, smiled at Alice's small smile and walked away with as much dignity as a runny nose would allow. *Well! That was awkward.*

FORTY

The rest of the passengers seated at their group dinner table had finished dinner and were gathering in the social lounge one deck below. Alice and Victoria sat across from one another, and the waiter brought them a bottle of champagne. As he uncorked and poured, Victoria looked across the room and through the wrap-around windows where a portion of deck and thrashing waves could be seen. When the waiter left, Alice raised her flute.

"To our voyage, may it always be an adventure!"

"Cheers," Victoria said softly. "I must say, it looks like more storm is upon us. I suppose that qualifies as adventure though."

Alice looked out the same windows and frowned. "It does seem rougher than usual, doesn't it?" She took an over-large gulp of her champagne, nearly draining the glass.

Victoria watched her. "Well, then so shall I!" she said, tipping her glass upward until emptied. She reached for the bottle to pour them both some more.

She no sooner had poured the bubbling drink when all the lights in the dining room went dark. Soon, a shipman began lighting lanterns. An officer approached their table.

"Ladies, if I may make a suggestion?" He bowed.

"Certainly, Captain," answered Alice.

"We've a bit of rough stuff coming up in the next couple hours, so we're suggesting everyone return to their cabins and stay put. Wandering around this ship in a storm is best done by the Navy."

"Thank you, Captain."

"But why not take your champagne?" he said, taking the bottle out of the ice bucket. He picked up a fresh linen dinner napkin from the next table and swaddled the bottle carefully.

The two women nodded silently and Victoria held the bottle as one might a baby.

"Goodnight, Captain," they said in unison.

Once in the outer galley, they giggled and held onto the railing for their footing. The ship was rolling on the waves fairly hard now.

As they walked down the long hall, Alice stopped outside Cabin 11.

"Would you care to come in for a drink?" she asked.

"I really should probably go back to—well, allright, maybe just another glass. No need to waste Dom Perignon."

Once inside, Victoria took possession of the only chair, leaving a smallish divan for Alice. The lights were also out in Alice's cabin, so she lit a candle lantern. It threw a strange and constantly moving series of bizarre shadows upon the walls. Victoria was mesmerized in a dizzying kind of way.

They sat across from one another.

"What are you looking at?" Alice asked.

"The shadows. They're quite disorienting, actually. I don't know why I keep looking."

"I know how to fix that." Alice moved to one end of the divan. "Come here, Victoria. Sit on this side with me."

Victoria stood to walk toward the divan when suddenly the ship lurched and threw her unceremoniously right onto Alice, who laughed. Then the lantern went dark.

Victoria righted herself but sat right alongside Alice.

"You're trembling." Alice placed her arm around Victoria's shoulder.

"I guess I'm a bit frightened. Of the storm, I mean."

Alice remained quiet. Then: "I guess I am too."

"It's unnerving, isn't it," said Victoria moving closer.

"Quite."

Alice turned toward Victoria and inclined her head. She could feel the warmth of Victoria's breath. She reached up and stroked her cheek, then her neck. She leaned in further and their lips touched. Lightly she brushed hers across Victoria's. Her fingers traced the outline of an ear, and then her mouth followed. She kissed each section, beginning with the lobe. She ran her tongue alongside the outer ridge until her tongue, damp and thick, slipped inside Victoria's ear and feathered the sensitive skin inside. She heard a moan. Victoria turned her body inward, toward Alice and placed her arms around Alice's neck.

"What are you doing?" she whispered. "What are you doing to me?"

"Everything, my Allure...everything I can, everything you'll let me."

"Alice?"

Alice murmured something.

Victoria pulled back, but she reached up and took Alice's face in her two hands, and held it still. They kissed again...and again.

"Ah...Good Lord, yes, Jack, yes."

***

The storm, at first startling but unthreatening, an inferior divinity of mere restless intensity, brought air saturated with anticipation. Fortune transmutable and tricky was soon thrashing around the ship like a demon-lover. The sighs and prayers and dreams of heaven began heaving and crashing over the bow of crushing virtue. The ship gave way to waves of water washing over the decks, engulfing the side-by-side barbettes, threatening to shatter the windows. Inarticulate sounds rose from the depths, the ominous music of appetite saturating surfaces, seeping into crevices unexplored. The bucking and lurching intensified with every wave, the sea crying loudly to suck the fullness inside its dark and swirling tunnels of watery depths, to sate its ironic thirst and feed the famished hunger of its own full heart. The scowling clouds, the pummeling of the waves and the craven howling of the skies as they unleashed rain and lightning and thunder from above, soaked and flashed and clamored for release. And then, at the edge of a vanishing storm plunged a final, stinging shaft of lightning. The shuddering vessel trembled as a shivery wind blew across the flat planes of her curves and around and around her obstructions, still fierce, its volume sacred, its splaying of every grand opening a shock until it was warmed, and wet, and slipping around and around, in and out. The blessed moment of release released. Deliverance delivered. Satiation sated. Everything took on the glow of a ghostly presence-chamber...for royalty perhaps. And then...and then the lessening...plateaus of momentary calm catching purchase in the slower heaving, the slacking of wind and noise, the fast collapsing fury and the mere whimpering rain.

Soft, plump, salty tears of rain.

FORTY ONE

Lady Victoria slept soundly for the better part of four days upon her return to England. She was tended to by her brother's staff, but she had the same bedroom suite as when her father was alive and master of the family. Her sister ensured that no one but herself and the household help were allowed in Victoria's rooms. Each day for a week, a fresh bouquet of Victoria's favorite flowers were delivered to the house without a card or note. Her sister Alexis had the bouquet placed closer and closer to Victoria's bedside, until finally the warrior managed to sit up in bed. She refused the offer of food, but after a while she asked for a cup of tea. And as the maid brought a pot of the steamy stuff on a tray with scones, butter and marmalade, Victoria decided she might have an appetite after all. Alexis set the example by making sounds of satisfaction with each bite of scone.

"I can't begin to imagine what you've been through, love."

"I can't begin to imagine telling you," Victoria said, between bites.

Their silence was interrupted by a loud guffaw, followed by choking sounds. Alexis jumped up in alarm, but Victoria stopped choking of her accord. She pointed at the flowers.

Alexis shrugged. "So am I to believe that despite the military nature of that awful ship that brought you home, that you, in fact, had at least one lovely...evening...or so?"

Victoria looked out the window. An early morning frost had covered the lower portion of the large bay windows she had loved all her life. Her window of dreams. "Or so," she answered giving her sister a sweet smile.

Alexis smiled back and began tidying up the service tray. "Good! Because she sends 'round a note every day inquiring after your well-being, and frankly, Luv, the staff thinks I have a secret suitor, and I'd like to nip that notion in the bud. At least until I actually do have a suitor," she added.

"You will, darling, you will. Have you answered her back at all?"

"Yesterday. I finally sent a note saying you were beginning to stir. Well, you were, a bit."

"I was dead to the world until this morning," Victoria said.

"Yes, but I know you, and I knew you'd come back to the land of the living sometime today."

"Maybe it was the scent of the flowers." Victoria reached over and picked up a petal that had fallen on her nightstand. She held it up to her nose and breathed it in.

"Maybe," said Alexis. "Allright, I'm off. I've got some

errands to do and—"

"Like what?"

"Well, I'm to have a fitting at the dressmakers. My winter clothes are disgraceful and downright baggy."

"You've lost weight," observed Victoria. "Is there someone you're meaning to impress?"

Alexis picked up her satchel and leaned down to kiss her sister. "I mean to do exactly that," she laughed, "just as soon as I find him!"

Alone in the softly-lit room, Victoria rested her head against the pillows Alexis had propped up for her. She remembered Alice's kisses. Her touch. Her reassuring voice. She tried to recall her first feelings of falling into the arms of her lover, that evening, after the dinner...she tried to call up the exact moment Alice's kiss had meant something different than before. She tried, but the feel of Alice's mouth upon her own, hard, insistent, urgent, in the darkened berth on the ship was the last flutter of thought she had before falling soundly asleep again.

FORTY TWO

"Come in, come in niece!" Queen Victoria waved away Victoria's half-hearted curtsy and pointed to a seat on the davenport. Next to Alice, whose face remained implacable but whose eye showed a fevered excitement.

"How are you, Auntie?" asked Victoria.

"I'm probably going to kick the proverbial bucket sometime soon, my dear, but until I do, Jack here has information on the scoundrels who are trying to hasten my demise! I shouldn't wonder but I might end up thanking them, but Jack won't hear of it!"

"Nor I, Auntie! What news have we then?"

"You tell her, Jack," said the Queen. "I'm tuckered out, and, say, Arthur?"

A male figure leaned out of the shadows. "Ma'am?"

"Half a brandy!" She cocked her ear to hear his movement but heard none. "It's quite allright, Arthur. I'm

202

to bed within a quarter hour. I promise," she added with a squeak.

Arthur brought the Queen her drink and served Victoria and Alice flutes of champagne.

Alice glanced at Victoria with a smirk and raised her glass in a mock salute. "Ah, champagne. It's been...so long."

Victoria ignored her and worked hard to keep the corners of her mouth from turning into a full grin.

"Jack, the news!" reminded the Queen. "Tell my niece the news!"

"Well, to make a long, complicated, treacherous tale of espionage short—"

"Yes, please," snipped Victoria.

The Queen looked back and forth between the two of them but said nothing. For once.

Lord, will Jack ever tire of adventure? She could get herself killed!

"It turns out that the target was not, apparently, your auntie," said Alice. "Your Majesty," she corrected, adding a nod. "While the Queen was in Ireland, someone tried to kill the Prince of Wales!"

"Bertie's quite good, by the way," said the Queen, addressing Victoria. "Not a scratch on him. But I'm not overly fond of Belgium at the moment!"

"Thank God," said Victoria. "So...? Ireland was...pleasant?"

"Ireland is always pleasant," said the Queen. "It's the food I have the most trouble with. Tasteless, on balance."

"Hmm. Of course, they think the same of us, Auntie," ventured Victoria.

"I'm well aware of what they call me, Niece!" She dithered around with some papers on her lap. Her voice was a hoarse whisper when she added, "I will simply say I have made some dreadful mistakes. There are no words for what I allowed, so we shan't go down that lane at this time. I haven't the energy to make the return walk."

"Auntie?" ventured Victoria. "Did you receive my letter?"

"Yes, what is this 'unpleasant and unsavory' information you wish to impart? Your letter was most obtuse, young lady. And, as even Bryant-Wincek noted, all war is unpleasant and unsavory."

"Bryant-Wincek, Auntie?"

The Queen gave a small cough and thumbed through a few more papers. "Don't see as well as I ought," she muttered. "Evelyn Bryant-Wincek is my new Personal Secretary. Benson's left, no notice to speak of. Well, I have reason to think he left one step in front of the law, but no matter, Bryant-Wincek doesn't hover."

"Well, you see," Victoria said, oblivious to the irony and scooting to the edge of her cushion to arrange herself in a most unladylike manner, "that's just it, Auntie! It is an atrocious war. But within it, our leadership in Africa have penned in the wives and children of the enemy and are keeping them in most unpleasant circumstances. It's not right, is it?"

"What do you mean 'penned up' child?"

"They are in concentrated camps! That's what they are called. I believe Lord Kitchener has called for it. But the people have inadequate clean water, no decent housing, not enough food and almost no medical care."

"I'm led to understand they prefer it that way, niece!"

"Well, they can't possibly, Auntie! The women's children are dying before their very eyes. The conditions are quite bad, I assure you. They do have some old country remedies they prefer to use on some ailments, but these are illnesses they are not familiar with and there are plenty who would accept good medical help."

"Well, I'll take it up with my advisors," the Queen said. "But you know these things take time. So I'll appoint you as a royal emissary to the Army Nursing Service, which—"

"Auntie, no! That is, thank you dearly, Auntie, but then I'd have to wear those awful matron clothes, and that entire nursing system needs to be modernized."

"Oh well, in that case, why didn't you say so sooner? I'll put Lenchen in charge of that...and you'll help, won't you? We'll look into this situation down in Africa."

"Yes, cousin Lenchen would be ideal," said Victoria.

"Jack, there is something important I need to discuss with you," the Queen said. Dormier sighed. "It might involve you, too, niece."

"Certainly Ma'am," said Alice.

"I'm going, per my usual Christmas sojourn, to Osborne House next month. I'm requesting you and my niece to join the family."

Both young women looked stunned. Invited? Together? Impossible!

"I would prefer, however, if you both would not speak of this to anyone, and if you would simply follow along in a separate vessel. We'll hire one for you as I don't want anyone to suspect you are accompanying me. For security reasons, you understand."

"Do we have any reason to suspect anyone has untoward inclinations with regard to your well-being, Ma'am?" It was Alice leaning forward to speak now.

"We always have reason to suspect exactly that," the Queen said. "But...but, yes, perhaps more reason than usual. I'm not well—you surely have surmised as much, and I'm uneasy with the sudden departure of Benson. Something's amiss with that man, and I'm not sure what. I want to be careful."

It was late October 1900. Alice looked thoughtful. "So, you'll be leaving for Osborn House on December 20th?"

"Earlier this year...around the 16th....but my public schedule will say the 20th."

Everyone became quiet. The Queen closed her eyes, and Alice and Victoria looked at one another.

"Auntie?"

"Wha—Where am I?" the Queen asked. She seemed disoriented and tired.

Arthur emerged from the shadows again. The Queen's lady's maids were with him. "A bit late, Ma'am" cooed Arthur. "Past time for your nap."

Alice and Victoria stood while they wheeled the Queen out in her chair. A majordomo showed them out, and Alice turned to Victoria.

"I think we should have a strong pot of tea after that, don't you? You can come in my carriage, and I'll have my driver take you home after."

Victoria nodded. She felt numb. Auntie was weakening in front of her eyes.

Alice looked at Victoria, then she reached over and took her hand. They rode in silence to Alice's. Finally, Victoria spoke.

"I'm going to lose her, Jack...and soon. There's no need for anyone to take her life, it's ebbing away as we speak."

"I know, darling, but if we go, it might lift her spirits."

"Yes, I think it would." Victoria sighed. "I wouldn't mind having mine lifted a bit."

Alice smiled and put her finger to her lips. "When we're alone," she whispered, "totally alone."

Alice put her hand up to her forehead.

"Tired, sweetheart?" asked Victoria. "Oh my, you suddenly look too pale!"

"I suddenly don't feel well, at all, darling, and I—" With those words, Alice Ponsonby fell onto Victoria. Her body hot from fever, her skin white as a ghost.

FORTY THREE

Victoria paced outside the library, preferring the long hallway to the confined space of the reading room. It had been over an hour since the physician arrived. Alice's parents were with her, and Victoria resented their privilege of access and her lack of it.

It's not fair. I am her betrothed. But do they know that? Did she tell them? If they know, do they object? She is the granddaughter of an earl...but I'm in line for the throne! Well, all right, that's pretty much fiction and will never happen...

Victoria recognized her own petulance and knew herself well enough to know it was fear. The panic quickly followed, but panic was a mere vehicle for terror. She sat down on a hallway bench. She tried to calm herself, but the best she could master was to stay still. The click of the door handle brought her to her feet.

Alice's parents walked toward her slowly. Victoria saw that her mother's face was tear-stained and her father's nose was brick red. They removed the masks they wore, and placed them in a small receptacle outside Alice's door.

Alice's mother, who had been her own mother's best friend, took Victoria's hands. "She has typhoid fever. She's on quinine, she—"

"Is it contagious?" interrupted Victoria. "I must see her!"

"Yes, you must," agreed Lady Ponsonby. "We want you to be with her as much as possible. No, it's not contagious. Please...please help her."

Victoria looked at her, startled. *Had Alice said anything about the Magick? But...but she hadn't told Alice, yet. She planned to tell her, soon. But...*

Lord Ponsonby cleared his throat. "I, uh, that is to say, Alice's mother and I, give our full blessings to, uh, to you and Alice." He seemed relieved to have got it out and was inspired by his success to say more. "Really, Victoria, as long-time friends with your mother, we would be honored to consider you our daughter...too!"

Victoria nodded, and as they seemed to need it, she hugged both of them. "I'd like to see her...will the doctor be in there long?"

"Not too very," said Lady Ponsonby. At that moment, the doctor came out of the room.

"She'll have some relief soon," he said. "The malarial treatment will make her sleepy, of course. I'll want you to monitor her temperature. It may go up or down a point, but any more than that, I'm to be called immediately. For now, she can stay at home. Also, if she seems at all delirious, that's not good. I'll want to be called. Otherwise, I'll be back this evening."

The Ponsonbys walked him to the door, and Victoria slipped into Alice's bedroom. A small lamp opposite the bed was lit, but the blinds were closed and the room remained otherwise dark.

"It's the terrible headache, darling, that's why it's so dark," Alice whispered.

Victoria knelt down alongside her bed and took her hand. "Shhhh, darling, keep your eyes closed and sleep a bit. I'll be here when you awaken. I promise."

"Not ready to die, to leave you," whispered Alice. Her eyes closed and she was asleep.

"Not going to allow that to happen, sweetheart," whispered Victoria. She stayed on the floor by the side of the bed until Alice appeared to be in a deep sleep. She rose, walked to the window and peeked out through a wooden slat. It was rainy and windy outside. Londontown was beginning to float in a thickening fog.

Victoria sat down at the table with the small lamp and foraged through her carpetbag. She thought to bring a change of clothing, a notebook and a book. She also had a small bottle of brandy in her satchel. She opened it and took a swig. More tired than she realized, and confounded about what to do next, she fell asleep in the chair. A single light tap on the door awakened her. She opened the door and stepped into the hallway.

"We've a second room that opens into Alice's," said Lady Ponsonby. "I've had them make a dinner for you. If you'll have a light bite to eat in there while they move a small chaise into Alice's room, you can sleep quite comfortably with Alice...I mean, in her room, I mean—oh, dear, nothing's coming out right."

Victoria had no idea who "they" were, but she nodded her assent to the nourishment, the closeness, everything.

"Thank you.

Lady Ponsonby opened Alice's door, and Victoria followed. Once in, a second door was opened from the other side by a maid who glanced past them at Alice.

"Alice used this as her study," said Lady Ponsonby.

Victoria sat down at a small table in Alice's study, but when she realized she could not see Alice from her position, she moved the table and her chair to be in sight of Alice's bed.

She watched, numb to her own feelings, as the maid refreshed the water pitcher in Alice's room. Two housemen quietly carried in a small but comfortable, upholstered chaise longue and placed it near the window. The maid put two coverlets and several pillows on it. She also moved the small table with the lamp closer to the chaise. By the time they were finished, Victoria had eaten. Mostly, she drank two large goblets of cold water. But she had a piece of sliced chicken and a couple sections of orange. It was all she could manage.

When everyone was gone, Victoria positioned herself in a sitting up position on the chaise, two pillows behind her and the third pillow placed on her lap. She opened her notebook and set it on the pillow. She thought that staring at the blank page might allow her to recreate the eight steps. She racked her brain trying to remember the eighth one. The healing was largely dependent on steps one through seven, but she recalled something about the eighth step was important.

She looked at the blank page. She focused hard on the picture in her mind, willing the image of her mother's beautiful cursive to appear.

Step One. Clear your mind of all thought; slowly let in the destination of your focus. *That's easy!*

Victoria squinted at the blank page. Step Two seemed blurry. She focused. The handwriting finally appeared, although it seemed a shade lighter than Step One.

Step Two: With the mirrors, create the second impression with your mind first and then project it onto the universe and alongside the original object. *Ah, easy enough! That's what I did with the German airship!*

Step Three: With the crystal, close your eyes and then go deep inside the wound; open your eyes once inside the wound. *Yes, exactly! I did that with my shoulder and with Dirk's father's wound.* She frowned at the thought of Dirk the son...surely, she could have done nothing there. He had lost his legs. And much blood...surely...

Step Four: Stay there, make your presence known, touch every nerve, every fiber of vessel, muscles, tendon, bone and every drop of blood. *Yes, yes, I did that.*

Victoria continued to stare at the blank page, her mother's words visible and familiar to her. The handwriting...her mother had elegant penmanship. And her choice of words! Victoria smiled. Her mother always wanted to say things simply but precisely.

Step Five: When you are done, go back and do the same again, watch for crevices where illness hides and even layers of normal looking things under which disease can camouflage itself; crawl into these dark places and shine a light. *Hmmm, I may have missed this one.* She began to wonder if Dirk's father had survived after all. He seemed cured—weak but mobile.

Step Six: Talk to the wound now cleansed of disease. Reassure the wound it will soon be healed completely. *Hmm, well, I believe I did a version of this, yes, I meditated, I sat very still...did I talk to the actual wound though?*

Victoria began to see that she had skimped somewhat on the directions so far. Daddy said it wasn't easy. He made a point of saying it.

Step Seven: As you leave the wound create an impression of the healing in your mind; once you have exited the wound, a great calm will inform you the healing has taken place. *All right, good. I did that one. I did feel the sense of calm, although I thought I was a bit depressed! Maybe calm feels that way sometimes.*

Victoria scanned the blank notebook sheet. Nothing. No Step Eight. The other steps had shown up on the page with only a slight blurriness, which was soon put in focus. But Step Number Eight was nowhere to be seen. She reread the first seven steps. She was certain she had memorized it. She was positive. So she sat back in the chair and closed her eyes. She conjured up the day Daddy had shown her the note. She looked at it now, with eyes closed and slowly began to see every written word. When she got to Step Eight, she saw it, plain as day. At once amazed and relieved, she read it aloud.

Step Eight: In this situation, you will need to use both the mirrors and the crystal. If you have exited the wound and are not as calm as your wisdom tells you is possible, project the second, healed impression, alongside the original wound or person. *This!* This was what she feared most—that she would leave the wound and still not feel good about things.

Her eyes slowly scanned the rest of her mother's instructions.

"In these cases (may they be few), your initial uncertainty may cause a delay in awareness of the healing. You must wait for a sign of healing, which

usually will come from the person who has received it.

"In that transference, the healing is then given back to you so that you may be reminded that wisdom is neutral, without agenda, without bias. Wisdom can flow from you and to you; only fear and uncertainty can delay the flow.

"This will convince you of the power of your Magick inasmuch as fear and uncertainty caused you to doubt it. Try not to doubt it, but if you do, the Eighth Step is the solution. Still, as one who loves you unconditionally, I must warn you: Never use the power to gain what you want for someone who loves you if you do not love the same in return. It could cause great harm.

"Darling daughter, read this several times, memorize it, burn it; only you can transfer the Magick to another, and that must be one of your own blood, however close or distant. Next, mind that you mustn't ever misuse the Magick to cause death, pain or suffering to another; if you have, that Karma will be revisited upon you unless you have cleansed your own wound of pride. Think on this with concern so that a healing you wish to effect does not fail for lack of your own harmonic balance. Your loving Mumsi."

Victoria blinked and stared at the blank page again. *The Kaiser's airship!* She had caused a great deal of damage...and pain. She had misused the Magick! She could not afford to make such an error with Alice. Victoria shivered and drew the blanket up around her chin.

She was startled when a voice from across the room called to her.

"Victoria? Victoria, darling, I'm slipping away...I'm trying not to..."

Victoria rushed to her side, felt her brow and knew her fever had risen alarmingly high. She went in search of the Ponsonbys, who immediately summoned the doctor. While they were in with their daughter, Victoria slipped out the front door.

FORTY FOUR

Every day for nine days, Victoria stood on the corner nearest the Ponsonby residence. She waited until she saw the doctor exit his carriage. As long as he was still coming to see Alice, she was alive. Dressed in her urchin clothing, no one from her set would recognize Victoria.

She walked for miles every day. She couldn't explain her actions to herself and dared not try to explain them to anyone else. Did she not believe in their love? Did she not believe in her own powers? She walked past shops filled with Christmas decorations and gifts, but she felt no joy. Her family knew something was wrong, but they left her alone. Even Alexis just looked at her curiously. They knew about Alice. They knew Victoria was not going to visit her. Notes from Lady Ponsonby were left unopened in the plate in the foyer—unopened, unread, unwanted. She'd never be able to face them again. And Alice...if Alice survived....Victoria tried not to take that thought to its natural tragic conclusion. Alice would never want to see her again, she knew that.

She visited the boys and girls near the wharf. They all asked about Jack. *Jack went to Africa. Should be back soon. Will tell him you lot are asking after him. He'll be happy to hear that. Wait! David Dockwall? Arrested? For trying to steal the Queen's jewels when they were sent out to be reset? How on earth would Dockwall know when that might be? Well. Good. I hope they locked him up. A year! Not nearly long enough. Here, a few quid for some treats. No, no, don't worry...mind you, pass the treats around fairly. Just as Jack would have done. Goodbye, now. Yes, I'm well, thank you. See you next time.*

She didn't even know why she had gone to the wharf. Needed something familiar, she supposed. As she was nearing her family home one afternoon, she almost ran headlong into Lieutenant Montgomery, walking arm-in-arm with a man.

"Oh heavens!" Montgomery said. "Victoria Dormier!"

"Hello, Lieutenant...er...well, how are you?"

Montgomery appeared flustered. "This is my husband, Ted Sharpe."

Victoria shook hands with the gentleman, and they all stood awkwardly on the corner.

"Well, is everyone else home on leave?" asked Victoria. "I've not heard a thing since returning."

Julie Montgomery glanced at her husband. "Oh, you haven't heard, have you. Of course not."

"Heard what?"

"Jones is still there and fine as far as I know, but Captain Privet is back with a minor wound that has her at recovery in Aldershot."

"Oh dear! Can she have visitors?"

"Uh, yes, of course. I think it would be a capital idea if you would go see her. She's...you know, I think I'll let her tell you. Say, we're just on our way to meet my parents for tea, but...uh, lovely running into you."

Montgomery's husband tipped his hat and after the hasty goodbye, Victoria walked slowly toward her house.

***

When she saw the solemn grey building, there wasn't a person in sight. She walked inside and up to the reception station. The interior did not disappoint the exterior. Long grey hallways led to right angle turns; one imagined there was nothing good around those corners.

The staff directed her to a tree out on the expansive lawn where two chairs were placed half in the sun, half under an awning of leafy shade. Privet was seated in one of them, a notebook in her lap. She was dressed in her khaki uniform. The day was chilly, but Privet wore no coat.

"Hallo, Captain! Don't get up, please!" Victoria shouted as she approached her.

Privet looked at her blankly.

"Captain Privet?"

"Yes?"

Victoria was stopped cold by the apparent lack of recognition. "It's, uh, Dormier!"

Privet looked away but nodded.

"May I sit down?"

"If you wish."

Victoria sat in a lawn chair, pulled her coat close and looked to the sky. "Weather's going to be turning quite cold soon, I think."

"Dormier," said Privet, "if I want to discuss the weather, there's 100 people in various states of wounded in there who are constitutionally incapable of discussing anything *but* the weather," she waved toward the hospital.

"All right, then tell me what happened? I saw Montgomery and her husband in London yesterday. They told me you were here."

"What else did Monty tell you?"

Victoria shook her head, trying to remember. "Well, she said Jones is still there, and Monty apparently got married as she introduced him as her husband, and...what?"

"St. James didn't...didn't make it."

"What? Oh my God. How? What happened?"

Privet reached into her shirt pocket and pulled out a pack of cigarettes. She offered one to Victoria but only as a courtesy as Private Dormier didn't smoke. Victoria took one.

"I can't believe this," she said to Privet.

"Why not? It's a war. People die. St. James was tending to the wounded at the forward point, and they were completely surprised and taken over by Boers. We lost about 80 that morning."

Victoria dropped her gaze to the grass. St. James had been such a good physician. A good person, too. She acted a bit tough, but she was all heart. She wondered if Alice knew. Damn. Very bad, this whole idea of war. She chided herself for having taken it all too lightly before she went down to Africa.

"She saved Alice's life."

"Who? Oh. How is our dear Jack Pierce?"

"Not well," said Vitoria in a whisper. "She has

typhoid."

"Oh Christ. Bad that. I had a touch of it. Awfully sorry. I know you were keen on her."

"Well—well she's still alive, or was this morning," said Victoria.

Privet looked at her and nodded.

"I ever tell you the story of how I fell hard for Monty?"

"Oh. Oh, I'm so sorry. I didn't know. And now....oh."

"Yes, she's married. She was always going to get married. But I pushed her into it faster."

"Really?" Victoria was surprised. "How?"

Privet looked at her. Hard.

"Oh!" said Victoria. "Oh. Oh dear."

"Naturally it was the best two nights of my life, and maybe hers, too."

Victoria was impressed. "Two nights."

"But when it's not right for both, it's not right for either," said Privet.

Victoria looked off across the expansive lawn. Was that her problem, too? No...no my problem is—

"I'm sorry, Captain," she said, interrupting her own thoughts. "Awfully brave of you to give it a try though."

"Ha!" screamed Privet. "Me? It was her, you silly goose. I was willing, sure, but I didn't know how to bring it up. I teased her and joked but, nah, wasn't me that made the first move. 'Twas her."

"Why are you in here, Captain? What was your wound?"

"A broken heart," said Privet, a wry hint of truthfulness in her tone. "Technically, that mild case of typhoid I mentioned. Very mild. I got lucky."

They chatted a while longer, and then Privet stood up. "Walk me back to the front door, will you, Dormier? Or are you a Princess now?"

Victoria nudged her and grinned. "I'll always be Dormier to you, Captain."

When they reached the door, Privet straightened her tie and smoothed down the front of her pants.

"Dormier, I don't know what your problem is with Pierce...or Ponsonby...or both," said Privet, "but—"

"Both," Victoria said miserably.

"But I just have one thing to say to you. Whatever it is, if you love her and are loved by her, gather up your courage and go tell her."

"I can't. I left her while she was sickest. I might have been able to help her, I might have at least tried."

"Why didn't you?"

"I was afraid I wouldn't succeed. I was afraid I'd lose her anyway. That she'd die. That it wouldn't be enough. That—"

"Ha! But you have anyway. Lost her, I mean. Unless you go back. Then you really have failed. You'll lose her for sure if she doesn't die. And she might die, but she might not. Damn, if I had your attitude, I'd never have had the best two days of my entire adult life!"

"But you—" Victoria stopped herself.

"Lost her anyway? Yes, I did. But, you have to remember something, Dormier. Whether it's for a moment, a month or eternity, two hearts are better than one."

"Are you going to recover from...are you going to recover?" asked Victoria.

"I am," said Privet opening the door. "Your visit has helped me a lot. Thank you."

She stepped inside and closed the door quickly. Victoria watched through the windowpanes as Privet walked slowly down a long hall. She willed her to turn around, and when Privet did, Victoria smiled and waved. Privet waved back. Victoria had a sense of déjà vu, but shook her head and rushed to the train station to get back to London.

She closed her eyes and listened to the repetitive but somehow reassuring sounds of the train on the tracks. *Never use the power to gain what you want for someone who loves you if you do not love the same in return. It could cause great harm.* She understood now. She needn't have worried. She hoped it wasn't too late.

***

She knocked on the door and no one answered. She could see some muted lighting through the front windows. Another knock. Nothing. The panic rose up through her chest and seemed stuck between her heart and her throat. Desperate, she pushed on the door handle and stopped short when it opened.

She saw the Ponsonbys walking down the hall. Lady Ponsonby was drying her eyes and wiping off her cheeks. Victoria came to an abrupt halt. She was too late.

"Oh darling," said Lady Ponsonby, running toward her, "how can we ever thank you! We cannot! There is no way on earth. You are an angel!"

"Damn good job, damn good job," Lord Ponsonby said, his eyes rimmed red, his voice catching.

Victoria looked at them and began to cry.

"Oh darling, it's all right now. Her fever broke the day after...after you were here last, and each day she's grown stronger. She was asleep when we left her, but you go on in. She's asked for you every day."

Victoria nodded, speechless.

Jesus Christ! Scare me to death, why don't you!

Alice was asleep when Victoria knelt down beside her bed. She touched her arm, and then put her own head alongside it. She wept silently until the bed linens were damp beneath her face. She was so tired. So tired of resisting, figuring it all out, fighting it. She loved this woman, and she always would. She was her everything.

"I can't believe you left me when I was at my sickest," said Alice in a clear voice.

Victoria jerked her head up. "I...I...I—"

Alice sat up. "Come here, darling. I know. I know what you've been questioning. I understand, I truly do. And you did help with the healing. I know you did. I saw you reading your notebook. I saw you meditating. You think you left me, and you did, but you helped to heal me before you left."

"I did?" Victoria felt immediately guilty. "I really can't take any credit—"

"No, of course not, Treasure, but your uncertainty gave me the will to recover, to live, to love you forever. I knew you'd come back...I, well, darling, you know I deeply hoped it.

"Oh Jack!" They kissed long and sweetly. Then Victoria pulled back. "But your parents...they think I healed you!"

"I know," said Alice, grinning. "And that's just the way we want it! They were beginning to lose their faith in miracles. We've given it back to them."

"Well...well, I did go over all the steps...the healing notes my mother left me."

"Oh, in that notebook, darling?"

"Yes, darling."

Alice reached for something on her bedside table. "This notebook, darling?"

Victoria's eyes got wide. They both knew that notebook was blank.

"Yes, my heart, that's the one. Thank you so much for keeping it safe." She fairly whipped it out of Alice's hand.

"You're welcome, my love. I thought it might be something you'd need to refer to, now and then."

There was a knock on the door.

"Come in," said Alice. "Oh, Mummy, Daddy! I feel so much better now Victoria is here, and we're all together."

Her parents were gleaming. Then her father stepped forward, holding an old satchel.

"Just popped in for a second—didn't know if you'd still be needing these," he said.

Alice and Victoria fumbled with the closure buckles, and then they both looked inside the bag. It was all of Jack's clothing.

When they looked up, Alice's parents had slipped out of the room.

Victoria took the white silk scarf out of the bag. She put it around Alice's neck and pulled her close.

"I always loved that scarf on you, Jack."

"Thank you, Victoria." Alice reached up, took the scarf from around her neck and wrapped it around Victoria's body...and pulled her close. "Likewise, Treasure, likewise."

THE END

Afterword

No attempts were made on the life of Queen Victoria in 1900, although earlier in her reign, seven incidents took place. Some were clearly assassination attempts, others attempts to claim notoriety by the assailant. But the trip she took to Osborne House in December of 1900 was a final journey for Queen Victoria.

The Queen was steadily weakening, although her physician, who never actually saw the Queen disrobed, could find no one thing to account for her rapidly declining health. There were the usual ailments of old age, of course, but, in the end, the longest reigning Queen of England died in her sleep on January 22,1901.

One of her last requests was that her Pomeranian, Turri, be laid upon her deathbed. Victoria was 81 years old.

The Boers were eventually, but not at all quickly, defeated. The three-and-a-half-year war ended with representatives of Great Britain and the Boer states signing the Treaty of Vereeniging, which recognized British military administration over the Orange Free State and Transvaal.

The treaty also authorized a general amnesty for Boer forces. Black South Africans were specifically excluded from having political rights in the reorganized South Africa. And while England did succeed in establishing a single government rule in southern Africa, it did not eliminate Afrikaner nationalism. Historians usually agree that the Second Boer War emboldened, strengthened and secured Afrikaner ethnic identity.

The constitution was approved for the Union of South Africa, which combined the Transvaal and the Orange Free State, in 1910, by the British Parliament. It was a maledictory document of equivocation, compromise and irony-adjacent self-interest that kept the racial distinctions. It ensured white rule, which in turn set the stage for the establishment and ideologies of Apartheid. Within a few years, the Union of South Africa passed other laws severely limiting property ownership by all but the whitest and most wealthy South Africans.

As part of their overriding grievances, the Boers accused the British of war crimes during the conflict. Among the list of crimes, rape, torture and setting up concentration camps for the internment of civilians were tops on the list. Frederick Sleigh Roberts, 1st Earl Roberts, whose nickname was "Bobs," took over the command of the forces in South Africa from General Sir Redvers Henry Buller. Roberts felt the key to victory over the Boers was to strip the Boer guerillas of any ability to live off the land— to get food and supplies from their families. Roberts is generally credited with devising the idea of establishing military internment of the Boers' families. (He borrowed the concept from the almost concurrent Spanish-American War, 1898-1901, which had its origin in the Cuban Revolution of 1895-98.) Roberts also invoked the "scorched earth" tactics that were so famously intensified under his successor, Herbert Kitchener. As Commander-in-Chief of the British, Kitchener's merciless amplification and grim enactment of Roberts' blueprint was both brutal and ultimately successful.

"First, they chose an ill-suited site for the camp. Then they supplied so little water that the people could neither

wash themselves nor their clothes. Furthermore, they made no provision for sufficient waste removal. And lastly, they did not provide enough toilets for the overpopulation they had crammed into the camps." British Physician Dr. Henry Becker

The British government did not address the war crime allegations. Eventually, though, Sir Arthur Conan Doyle (yes, of Sherlock Holmes fame) took up the British banner is his book <u>The Great Boer War</u>, which he wrote in eight days and revised through 16 editions. But even he memorialized the great degree of difficulty Britain encountered.

"...the modern Boer—the most formidable antagonist who ever crossed the path of Imperial Britain. Our military history has largely consisted in our conflicts with France, but Napoleon and all his veterans have never treated us so roughly as these hard-bitten farmers with their ancient theology and their inconveniently modern rifles." Sir Arthur Conan Doyle

Although the Boer fighters were immediately set free after the war, their lands had been salted, burned and ruined for agrarian pursuits. Their wells were poisoned, their livestock was slaughtered and the homes and farm dwellings were looted then burned to the ground.

Lord Kitchener died in 1916 when a German U-Boat sunk his ship midway through World War I.

The idea of modern warfare, namely that begun on a grand scale during WWI, was born in the lessons learned from the Second Boer War. The British Commandos were fashioned after the oft-successful Boer Commandos, who engaged in guerilla tactics the British had never seen.

The bulky British weaponry of the Africa conflicts gave way to faster, more mobile and more deadly weaponry in WWI. Military medicine, practiced at a most elementary level in Africa, was enhanced, energized and sophisticated by physicians and nurses who had learned from the diseases and illnesses the British confronted in Africa. Finally, Britain realized its forces were woefully out of shape, physically, and their set-piece war tactics hopelessly deadly. By 1914 and the onset of WWI, the hard lessons learned in these and other areas during the Boer conflicts ensured a British force more prepared for war than it had ever been.

But proving once again that there is nothing quite like the indomitable spirit of those who will be heard, in 1994, The Republic of South Africa held its first universally free elections and Nelson Mandela was elected its first Black African President. The period of time from the Dutch East India Company landing at the Cape of Good Hope to the election of Mandela, who had been imprisoned for 27 years, was 345 years.

The Boer War, fought at a total expense of 210 million dollars, the most expensive war up to that point, would not be declared a British victory until 1902.

Great Britain brought more than half a million troops to the theater of war; the Boers had less than 90,000 fighting troops.

Nearly 100,000 people died during the Second Boer War, which lasted from 11 October 1899 to 31 May 1902. Nearly 20,000 Black Africans were killed, in battle and in the camps. About 20,000 British troops were killed, and another 30,000 were wounded; of those killed, nearly 14000 died from disease. Nursing staff from England,

Ireland, Australia and Canada died. Over 1000 Australians troops lost their lives, about 300 Canadiens perished and hundreds of Irish (some fighting for the British, others fighting for the Boers!) also died. Several thousand citizens of other countries fighting for both sides were killed.

The Boer losses were about 14,000 fighting troops, but about 26,000 Boer prisoners of war were sent to such far-off spots as Bermuda, India and Ceylon among other places. Almost 30,000 Boer women and children and elderly men (families of the Boer fighters) held in British concentration camps died from diseases caused by malnutrition, poor sanitation, inadequate medical help and minimal and inadequate housing. Social welfare worker and feminist Emily Hobhouse was finally able to bring British public attention to the plight of the Boer women and children in the camps after she made visits to several camps in January and February of 1901.

Also, over 300,000 horses died in the Boer War.

Prince Christian Victor of Schleswig-Holstein, "Christie" to his family, one of Queen Victoria's grandsons, her favorite, contacted typhoid and died of enteric fever a couple months before the Queen died.

The Queen was styled Her Majesty Victoria, by the Grace of God, of the United Kingdom of Great Britain and Ireland, Queen, Defender of the Faith, Empress of India. She was visited on her deathbed by the person she called "dear Willy," her German grandson, Kaiser Wilhem II, whose monarchy was abolished in 1919, several years after he launched Germany on a collision course with the world by a series of missteps that led to The First World War in 1914.

Wilhelm had a conflicted and stormy relationship

with his British and Russian cousins, and many other relatives from most of the monarchies in Europe, but he cared about his grandmother, Queen Victoria. As early as 1886, however, Wilhelm was suspected of having pro-Boer sympathies. Potsdam, near the German capital of Berlin, was a residence of many Prussian kings and the German Kaiser Wilhelm II, until 1918.

It was actually the British who used ballooning for reconnaissance during the Boer War—a role Germany was to fulfill to huge advantage later with their Zepplin airships during the early part of WW I. And motorcycles—yes, they existed but were not used in the Boer war cause. No record was found of any female physicians serving either side during the Second Boer War, although there were hundreds and hundreds of Nurses.

There were 40,000,000 casualties, military and civilian, in WW I, which began in 1914 and ended in 1918. Forty Million.

There were 80,000,000 military and civilian casualties in WW II, which began in 1939 and the Second Sino-Japanese War that began in 1937 and which is considered part of WWII. Eighty Million. Another 50,000,000 people have been killed in other wars and conflicts since the end of WWI. Fifty Million.

The total number of all peoples who died as a result of wars since the end of the Boer War is approximately 190,000,000. That is the current total population of Brazil.

One hundred ninety million humans have been lost to war since 1902 and millions more were wounded and maimed.

Except for the Introduction-Dedication and Afterword sections, The Girl With 2 Hearts is a work of fiction.

T. T. Thomas is the author of three novels, two novellas and numerous short stories. In addition to her most recent work, <u>The Girl With Two Hearts</u>, Thomas' prior full-length novel is <u>A Delicate Refusal</u>, July 2013. The novel explores the lives and loves of women in England just as WWI breaks out. It has been referred to as a kind of "Downton Abbey" for lesbians and others! The title is taken from a quote by Edmond Rostand, author of the play <u>Cyrano de Bergerac</u>.

Her first full-length novel, <u>The Blondness of Honey</u>, was published October 2012. The Blondness of Honey is an historical romance novel set in the 1890's that explores the love between two women.

In December 2012, Thomas released a novella, <u>Vivien and Rose</u>, a book "written by" by Laura Hastings, the heroine of Thomas' first full-length novel, <u>The Blondness of Honey.</u>

T.T. Thomas also wrote <u>Two Weeks At Gay Banana Hot Springs</u>, her debut novella (2012). Her second book, <u>Sex On A Regular Basis</u> (2012) is a collection of short stories. Each of the four shorts stories is also available separately: <u>The Guy in Frankie's Hatbox</u>, <u>Ronald Debby</u>, <u>My Second Stupid Suicide</u> and <u>Bread and Butter</u>.

In another life, Thomas was a newspaper reporter and editor, a contributor to various regional and national magazines, as well as public relations and publicity executive for her own and other international companies. For the past 18 years, she was the Finance Director at a Mercedes Benz franchise in Thousand Oaks, California.

Thomas is a member of Romance Writers of America (RWA), the Golden Crown Literary Society, Lambda Literary and numerous other writing groups. T. T. Thomas lives in Southern California. You can keep up on the author's latest news and books at <u>www.ttthomas.com</u>.